When he opened the front door and stepped inside, he came face-to-face with the masked man.

A quick scan of the room was enough to send him into full fight mode. Natalie was on the floor. Her neck was bruised. Her niece Shelly was nowhere to be seen.

A sudden quick punch hit Rick in the gut. He grabbed the man and smashed him into the wall.

"Where's the little girl? What have you done with her?" Rick got no answer. Just a cold stare from those deep brown eyes. Movement from where Natalie was had Rick turning to see if she was alright. The assailant took advantage of this temporary distraction and shoved Rick aside, then ran out the door. Rick wanted to follow but he couldn't risk leaving Natalie. Her injuries could be serious.

He rushed across the room and kneeled by her side. "Are you okay? Natalie, please wake up."

Natalie opened her eyes. She tried to speak but her voice was strained.

"Where's Shelly?" Tears streamed down her temples...

Addie Ellis lives in the Northeast with her husband, son and energetic little dog. She enjoys hiking and going to the beach with her family. Having been a teacher, she has a soft spot for children. And animals, too. For Addie, writing has become a way to find adventure while exploring new places.

Books by Addie Ellis

Love Inspired Suspense

Hunted in the Mountains
Hiding from Danger

Visit the Author Profile page at LoveInspired.com.

HIDING FROM DANGER

ADDIE ELLIS

INSPIRATIONAL ROMANCE

If you purchased this book without a cover you should be aware that this book is stolen property. It was reported as "unsold and destroyed" to the publisher, and neither the author nor the publisher has received any payment for this "stripped book."

MIX
Paper | Supporting responsible forestry
FSC® C021394

LOVE INSPIRED® SUSPENSE
INSPIRATIONAL ROMANCE

ISBN-13: 978-1-335-95750-4

Recycling programs for this product may not exist in your area.

Hiding from Danger

Copyright © 2025 by Addie Ellis

All rights reserved. No part of this book may be used or reproduced in any manner whatsoever without written permission.

Without limiting the exclusive rights of any author, contributor or the publisher of this publication, any unauthorized use of this publication to train generative artificial intelligence (AI) technologies is expressly prohibited. Harlequin also exercises their rights under Article 4(3) of the Digital Single Market Directive 2019/790 and expressly reserves this publication from the text and data mining exception.

This is a work of fiction. Names, characters, places and incidents are either the product of the author's imagination or are used fictitiously. Any resemblance to actual persons, living or dead, businesses, companies, events or locales is entirely coincidental.

For questions and comments about the quality of this book, please contact us at CustomerService@Harlequin.com.

® is a trademark of Harlequin Enterprises ULC.

Love Inspired
22 Adelaide St. West, 41st Floor
Toronto, Ontario M5H 4E3, Canada
www.LoveInspired.com

HarperCollins Publishers
Macken House, 39/40 Mayor Street Upper,
Dublin 1, D01 C9W8, Ireland
www.HarperCollins.com

Printed in Lithuania

Be strong and of a good courage, fear not, nor be afraid of them: for the Lord thy God, he it is that doth go with thee; he will not fail thee, nor forsake thee.
—*Deuteronomy* 31:6

In memory of my mother. She is missed by many.

ONE

The heat of the flames still burned under her skin. The nightmares continued to be so vivid. Natalie Owens stepped out into the cool night air, trying to catch her breath. She felt like she needed to be outside when she woke from one of the dreams that never let her escape. They kept her fighting to get out. They always ended with the groaning sounds the house made right before it collapsed with Natalie and her seven-year-old niece, Shelly, stuck inside. Tonight, though, there was something new that tore away the images and wrenched her from sleep. A shrieking that hadn't been there before. Not that night and never in her dreams. It left her feeling even more unsettled than usual.

She had rented this little cottage in a small mountain town near Catskill, New York, six months ago hoping to heal. To escape the nightmares. To find a way to live with what she lost that night. But nothing had changed. She walked farther into the yard, trying to breathe in the cool air and calm the pounding of her heart. Sometimes listening to the gentle sounds of the forest at night could distract her. Settle her emotions enough to keep from falling apart in front of Shelly. At twenty-seven years old, it sometimes felt like more than someone her age should be dealing with.

She was about to go back inside when a scream crashed through the soft rhythm of the woods, cutting over the rush of the river down the hill. It froze her in place. The sound of it. The absolute desperation in it. Like an echo of the shriek that tore her from sleep. Natalie was suddenly filled with the same intense panic that haunted her dreams. She edged toward the woods, trying to see down to the water. The rapids sounded rougher than usual tonight. It was too dark to see anything from where she was. She crept through the damp grass, letting it slip between her toes. The broken twigs and moist dirt grazed her skin as she entered the tree line. Inhaling the musty smells of things that hid in the shadows, she tried to consider that it could be some teens goofing around. It was late but some of the tourists were less attentive to what their kids did at night. Natalie couldn't imagine what else it would be.

The sky was cluttered with thick clouds from an approaching storm. She could smell the static-charged air. Rain was coming soon. The moon was mostly hidden, leaving the trees in a kind of darkness that made them all hover like shadowy figures looming over her. The chilly breeze coming off the river that cut through the land behind her house brushed over her skin, sending a hint of a shiver through her body. It was better than the heaviness of the heat that always burned through her after the nightmares. But she knew this shiver was from more than the cool night air.

Another scream shattered the soft tempo of the night, finally silencing some of the critters that she had heard most evenings without ever seeing them. But this was different. It sounded like someone yelled the word *no*.

She started moving faster, her heart bouncing deeper into her throat with each step. Was something wrong? Was someone hurt? The sound of gasps and movement on the surface of the water stopped her. Natalie considered the possibility that she was misinterpreting what she heard. That it could be something innocent. Young people playing around by the river's edge. It wasn't so long ago that it might have been her frolicking around in the water with friends. She leaned against a thick tree trunk, the rough bark scraping against her skin, and peered around it to get a closer look while hoping to avoid being seen.

A dark figure came running up the hill, snapping the fallen twigs lining the forest floor. Natalie's breath caught in her throat as she shifted back behind the tree. Why would someone be running through here this late? She took a deep breath and then dared to glance around the tree again. This time, the dark figure was much closer. As it ran by, Natalie realized she recognized those pajamas. The teddy-bear slippers on her feet. What was Shelly doing out here in the middle of the night? She knew better. Natalie had been clear about not leaving the cottage alone. They were in the middle of the woods. And they didn't know any of the people occupying the other cottages sprinkled in the trees around theirs.

Natalie took off running after her niece. She didn't have time to consider the reason for her being out here. The only priority was catching up to Shelly and making sure she was alright. It was her responsibility to look after her niece now that Natalie's brother and his wife were gone. That fire took so much. She couldn't lose Shelly now, too.

She called out. "Shelly! Wait!" She kept running. "Shelly, stop!" Natalie was able to slow down when Shelly finally stopped and turned toward her. The girl was still trying to catch her breath as Natalie approached. The terror etched in her niece's face made Natalie's heart skip out of her chest. Something was wrong. This wasn't just a child's folly. There was clearly more going on.

"What happened? Was that you screaming a minute ago?"

Shelly glanced down toward the water and then met Natalie's eyes. She nodded slightly. "There was a woman walking through the yard. I thought she was you. I know you go outside sometimes." Natalie waited, trying to be patient while Shelly seemed to try to collect her thoughts. "There was a man. He grabbed her and shoved her into the river. I saw her face right before she went under. I knew it wasn't you then, but I think he was hurting her." Her eyes welled up and tears spilled over. Her lips quivered in fear. It created a thick knot in Natalie's throat.

She pulled Shelly into her arms. "Did he hurt you?"

Shelly was shaking her head. "No. But that woman... He was holding her under. I was running back to the cottage to tell you." She sobbed. "I didn't know how to help her."

"It's okay. We'll call the police. Did he see you?"

Shelly stepped out of Natalie's embrace. "He turned around and stared at me when I screamed. He looked really angry. Like he was mad that I was there. Then I ran."

The sounds of heavy footsteps echoed through the trees. They were coming quickly. Natalie had to make a decision fast. She knew that the man would be looking for Shelly. She'd seen his face. Shelly said he'd looked angry. And was he really trying to drown someone? In this quiet little town? Their little rented cottage would be the first place he'd find. It was closest to where Shelly ran from.

They couldn't go back there. She pulled her niece on an angle the rest of the way up the hill. There had to be somewhere to go. A way to call the police. They couldn't run aimlessly around in the dark. Natalie wasn't wearing any shoes and Shelly wouldn't last long in slippers.

"Aunt Natty, what about that woman?" Shelly looked up at her in a panic, pulling her to a stop, her eyes wide with urgency. She seemed to expect Natalie to go back and do something. But that wasn't possible.

"I'm so sorry, but we can't help her right now. I have to get you somewhere safe. We have to keep moving. We'll call the police to help her, okay?" She pulled Shelly along, trying to put distance between them and the man from the river.

As they emerged from a dense cluster of pine trees, Natalie remembered an old log cabin she had seen on their walks in the first few months after moving into the cottage. It had always looked empty. Maybe they could hide there. They needed to find a phone. Most people kept landlines in the area, given how spotty the cell service could be. She started heading in that direction when Shelly stopped short, letting out a screech. Her niece pulled off her teddy-bear slipper and Natalie saw some blood trickling in the arch of her foot. There was no time to deal with that. Not with the sounds of branches and twigs snapping behind them as the man from the river seemed to be moving closer and closer. Natalie swooped Shelly into her arms and started running, ignoring the jabs of rocks and sticks into her feet. If Shelly hadn't been so small for her age, Natalie wasn't sure she'd have been able to carry her.

It was just a little farther. She had to get there before the man caught sight of them. The echoes of his heavy footsteps were getting closer. He must have heard Shelly's scream and turned in their direction. Maybe he heard the crunch of dead leaves and twigs as they had been running. Whatever was guiding him toward them, they were almost out of time. And, she realized now, if he was following their movements, how would the empty cabin be any safer than the cottage? Shelly was gripping the back of Natalie's neck, her eyes flooding with tears, as Natalie pushed harder. They were almost there. She could see the outline of the wood logs. The brick chimney above the roof. If only they could get inside and hide before that man cleared the trees and saw them.

A sharp pain shot through Natalie's toes, sending her stumbling forward. She fell to the ground, watching as Shelly tumbled under a wide bush, a harsh gasp escaping her throat. The sudden impact with the hard dirt knocked the wind out of her. She was nearly wheezing as she rolled over to look toward the pine trees. There was movement in the branches. He was almost out. Natalie turned and rose onto her knees as she tried to catch her breath. She had to get to Shelly. She had to keep going. Her eyes closed as the anguish started seeping under her skin. Her breaths were coming in painful gulps. *Lord, please help us. Show me a way out of this.*

Natalie opened her eyes and stumbled to her feet. She tried to ignore the stabbing pain in her toes and the burning in her lungs. She was about to reach for Shelly when snapping branches brought her head around to see the man pushing into the open. When lightning streaked across the sky, she could see that he was dressed in black from head to toe. A ski mask covered everything but the area around his eyes. She was pretty sure Shelly said she'd seen his angry expression. He had come prepared, then, with a ski mask in case he encountered anyone. He wasn't tall but the thickness of his build was intimidating. His wet shoes sloshed with each step he took. He was moving slower now that he could see Natalie. His head swiveled around. She presumed he was looking for Shelly. She took a step backward, trying to figure out her next move, when he started running toward her. Natalie reached for her niece, praying for the strength she needed, and pulled her from under the bush, then ran for her life.

Thunder rumbled through the house, pulling Rick Barrett from a deep, dreamless sleep. He was beginning to miss being back in his hometown. He had grown up in Phoenixville, Pennsylvania, and enjoyed a happy childhood, but couldn't seem to get himself to stay once he had been honorably discharged from the US Army. He missed seeing his parents and his sister, who all still lived there. He had even grown close to his brother-in-law. Rick had spent time in various places, trying to figure out what he would do with his life now. He decided to come to his family cabin in Maple Rapids to be by himself to think. The problem was that he wasn't alone nearly as much as he'd anticipated. Growing up spending his summers in the whitewater-rafting town, a little north of Catskill, he had become friendly with several of the locals. That made it difficult to keep to himself. Not that he didn't enjoy spending time with them. He just wanted a little more isolation to contemplate what was next for him. He had spent four years avoiding what he now knew he had to face in order to move forward.

Rick had served eight years in the army, five of them with the Special Forces. He had seen so much violence and cruelty in the world that it had become difficult not to see a potential threat in every stranger. Even after being out for a little over four years. He wasn't sure what he needed to do to move on but something had to change.

At thirty-one years old, Rick was ready to settle down and start a family. Not an easy task with the fear of losing anyone he might care about keeping him from opening himself up. He had lost some good friends during his time in the service. His difficulty trusting new people only compounded the situation. When he wasn't working or visiting with an old friend, he spent his time trying to seek guidance in prayer. He hadn't gotten any clear answers in the month and a half he'd been staying in the cabin, but he felt that the answers would come. He had always maintained his faith.

Rick jolted upright in bed when the sound of a woman's scream tore through the tedious thoughts that had been plaguing him for months. He quickly pulled on a pair of jeans and a T-shirt, then he took off to see if someone had been hurt. He dreaded what he would find. The idea of walking back into the darkness he'd left behind nearly made him hesitate as he opened the back door. A woman carrying a small child was rushing frantically toward his cabin in the pouring rain. He stepped outside, trying to see what they were running from. His heart began to thump in his chest in anticipation of what might await him on this stormy night. The sky was blank. Like a thick mass hovering over the earth, blocking the light from being able to touch any part of the forest around him. When he spotted a masked man dressed in black gaining on their position, it was obvious that the woman and child were in danger. The man's decision to cover his face made it clear he didn't want anyone to be able to identify him.

Addie Ellis

Rick didn't question what the man's intent would be once he caught his prey.

"Over here," he called to the woman. She looked up and saw him, then seemed to hesitate, slowing her pace. "Come inside." He wasn't sure she could hear him or if she would trust a stranger enough to go inside his cabin.

Both her and the child were in pajamas and drenched from the rain. The woman's feet were bare and covered in mud. The child she was carrying appeared to be a little girl. This wasn't the kind of thing that happened in Maple Rapids.

The woman turned to look over her shoulder, likely noting how close her pursuer was getting. Then she turned back to Rick with uncertainty in her eyes. He waved his hand, encouraging her to come to him. He walked farther into his yard. She moved toward him, continually glancing over her shoulder at the man chasing after her. Once she was close enough, he spoke to her.

"Go inside and lock the door. I'll deal with him." Rick could feel remnants of old instincts firing up. When she stopped just shy of the doorway, he told her again, "Take the kid inside. I'll handle things out here." Once they were inside, he turned to face the masked man, who was now no more than twenty feet away. He stopped and seemed to be watching Rick. Then he took a few steps forward. The black ski mask concealed most of the attacker's face. His black clothes made it difficult to discern his size in the darkness.

The man started walking slowly toward Rick. The closer he got, the more familiar he seemed. His stocky build was average. Rick could name twenty men he knew with the same frame. But there was something about his dark eyes. Was it possible he knew this man?

Rick took another step toward him. "What do you want with them?"

The masked man didn't answer. He continued slowly toward Rick until they were about five feet apart. The man kept looking at the cabin. He seemed intent on getting to the people inside. Rick wasn't about to let that happen.

When he focused on Rick, what little of his expression could be seen looked conflicted. As if maybe the two of them did know each other. "You need to step aside. Stay out of it," the masked man almost whispered, but with a deep growl. His voice was unrecognizable.

"That's not going to happen. You need to leave. I imagine she called the police. It won't be long before you won't have the option to go." Rick widened his stance, preparing for what might come. The rain poured down over everything. Thunder rumbled through him and lightning cracked across the sky. He wished he had put on shoes before coming outside.

The man stood a moment longer and then charged toward the door, trying to sidestep Rick. Rick threw his arm out, slamming it into the man's throat, throwing his own weight forward. They both spun around and crashed to the muddy ground. As Rick jumped back up, he could hear gasping from under the woven fabric covering the assailant's mouth. Then the man shuffled back and got on his feet. They stared at each other for a long moment before the attacker took a step forward. He rolled his head around, cracking his neck. It was something Rick had seen before from men who knew how to handle themselves and were gearing up to escalate things.

Rick wanted to turn to see what the woman and girl were doing. To verify that they were alright. He hoped the woman had locked the door, like he told her to. But he couldn't risk taking his eyes off the man in front of him to check. Rick could see his dark eyes peering through the small openings of the ski mask, seeming to assess him. The man felt vaguely familiar, but also completely foreign at the same time. Did it remind him of someone from his time with the Special Forces? Was it something else? Rick couldn't quite pinpoint it.

The assailant was very still. There was tension forming across his shoulders and through his arms, his fingers curling into fists. Then he charged forward, forcing Rick to push back hard. He quickly realized how solidly built his adversary was. Rick shoved with his entire body, his bare feet slipping on the wet ground. He inhaled deeply, slowing his heart rate, and dropped lower as he rammed his shoulder into the assailant's middle. A sharp grunt escaped the man's lips.

The rain was getting heavier, beating a steady rhythm against the leaves all around him. It was like pushing a brick wall, but Rick kept at it as their bodies locked together, neither of them willing to relent. Every move was met with a countermeasure most people wouldn't have had the skill to use. When the man stumbled over a tree root protruding from the wet soil, they both hit the ground and began to grapple in the wet grass. The slickness of the water made it difficult to get a solid grip on the guy.

Rick landed a punch but his fist slipped along the wet mask, shifting his weight off center. The man moved fast, trying to get an advantage as Rick's balance faltered. If only Rick could get that mask off. It didn't make sense that there was anything that felt familiar about someone who would be attacking people in the night. That simple thought distracted him for a moment too long and the assailant maneuvered behind him, trying to wrap his arm round Rick's neck. Rick slammed his elbow into the man's stomach with the kind of force only adrenaline could fuel. The man staggered away, gasping for air.

Rick jumped up ready for more but the assailant ran, partially bent over with his arms around his middle, into a dense patch of pine trees. Rick was about to follow when he heard the child sniffling over the buckets of rain beating down on everything around him, bringing his focus to the woman standing with the little girl at her side just outside the open doorway. He couldn't risk leaving them alone. What if that man circled back while Rick was running in the wrong direction?

The woman was staring toward the trees the assailant had disappeared into, then turned toward Rick as she lifted the little girl into her arms. Her eyes were sort of vacant. Probably the shock of it all. Her wet shorts and T-shirt were sagging over her skin. Rivulets of water slipped from her hair and streamed along the soft curves of her face. What had happened to them tonight before they made it here? He started walking toward them when sounds from within the trees stopped him in his tracks. He spun around. Had the masked man already come back? Rick didn't think he'd give up easily, but he certainly didn't think he'd be back so soon. He scanned his surroundings, then another sound helped him locate the area. He watched intently, waiting. For what, he wasn't certain.

TWO

Natalie watched the man standing in the rain and wondered what would happen if the masked man came back. Shelly wrapped her arms more tightly around her. Natalie had stepped outside when she saw the assailant running into the trees. She wasn't sure if she should stay in the stranger's cabin or try to make it back to her cottage. She hadn't found a phone inside. The crack of a branch had her stepping farther inside again, but the man who'd fought the masked man stood firm. Nothing seemed to frighten him. Then a small pack of deer came racing out of the forest into the yard. Something had spooked them— no doubt, the would-be attacker.

The man turned and hurried over to them. "We should get inside and call the police." She followed him in and watched him lock the door.

She couldn't help but wonder how he had learned to fight with such force. And more importantly, if they were safe with him. Natalie carried Shelly to the other side of the kitchen island, limping along slowly through the dark room. She didn't get the sense that he was dangerous. At least not to them. Still, she felt the need to have a little space between them. The interior of the cabin was well-kept. It was small with minimal furniture. There appeared to be two bedrooms with a bathroom in between that ran along one side.

The man walked slowly toward them. "Are you alright?"

As Shelly curled tighter into her arms, Natalie nodded, unable to find her voice. She was still processing everything that had just happened and the fact that neither of them had called the police yet. "You live here? I thought this place was empty." For some reason, that was the first thing that tumbled from her lips.

"It is most of the time. The cabin has been in my family for years. We don't use it as often as we used to. I came up a little over a month ago." He looked her over, seeming to check for injuries. His green eyes halted on her foot. "Are you hurt?"

She looked down to see the mud and what might be blood caked around her foot. She realized she was in some pain but the adrenaline was still staving off what would inevitably become much worse. A streak of lightning lit up the room, sending a jolt of anxiety through Natalie's body. She let Shelly down so she could get a better look at her foot. A moment later, the lights came on and she looked up to see the man walking over from where he flipped the switch.

"Would you mind if I take a look?" He nodded toward her foot. Thunder reverberated through everything as he stepped closer. He seemed to be scanning every little cut and scrape along her arms and legs. His eyebrows were drawn close together. His expression was kind of intense. She hadn't even felt most of the cuts happen.

"I'm Rick Barrett. You're safe with me. Can you tell me what happened?" He took another small step toward them. His deep voice held kindness. It eased a little of the tension tightening her body. When she didn't react, he continued until he was in front of her.

"I'm Natalie Owens and this is my niece, Shelly. Thank you for stopping him. I think he would've killed us." She felt her body tense again saying those words. "He may have drowned someone in the river." She started to step out from behind the kitchen island and stumbled.

Rick quickly moved to her side and steadied her with an arm around her waist. "What did he do to you?" He supported her as she limped over to the couch.

"I hit my toes on something and fell. That's how he caught up with us."

Rick eased her down onto the couch. Shelly climbed up next to Natalie and pressed herself close to her side. "I couldn't find a phone. I wasn't able to call the police." She watched him, hoping he would make the call. That he didn't have his own sinister intentions. Natalie wasn't exactly in the position to be able to run again, let alone fight someone his size. He was definitely over six feet tall and well built in an athletic way. From what she saw when he fought the masked man, he was agile and skilled. It made her wonder, again, why that was.

Rick grabbed a clean dishrag from the kitchen and wet it, then kneeled down in front of her. "I'll call the police in a minute. I want to see how serious your injuries are. Is this okay?" When Natalie nodded, he started to clean the blood and dirt from her skin. She winced a few times but didn't pull away. He carefully moved each of her toes. "I don't think anything is broken, but your toes are probably sprained given the bruising and mild swelling." He nodded toward Shelly. "Is she hurt?"

"She cut her foot when we were running. And I dropped her when I fell but she seems okay." Natalie turned to Shelly. "Are you in any pain?" Shelly shook her head and buried her face into Natalie's side.

"Can you tell me what happened? Who that guy was?" Rick looked Natalie directly in the eyes. His dirty blond hair fell across his forehead and he reached up, pushing his fingers through it. Now that he was close and everything was still, she couldn't help but notice the strong angles of his handsome face and the way his thick brown eyelashes curled over the lids of his soft green eyes. Eyes that seemed to hold so much intensity.

"I don't know who he is. Shelly saw him push a woman into the river." She paused for a moment, trying to gather herself. "I didn't see him or the woman. All I know is Shelly came running from the river and when she told me what happened, we ran. She'd seen him looking at her when she screamed. He must've had a mask with him. By the time he caught up with us, he was wearing it. I would have gone to my cottage but I thought he'd go there first. He must have heard us running." She stopped again, her voice catching. "I'm so sorry we got you involved."

"Don't be. You wouldn't have made it much farther before he caught up. He's strong and fast. I haven't come up against many people that could challenge me the way he did." He finished wiping her wound and stood up. "The phone is in the bedroom. I'll go call the police. Then I'll bring out some Band-Aids for her foot." He glanced at Shelly, then back to her. "And yours. Just give me a minute." Then he went into one of the bedrooms.

Natalie considered leaving but then heard him talking on the phone. He had it on speaker and she could hear both sides of the conversation. At least most of it. When the man on the other end told Rick they'd send someone over, he hung up and went into the bathroom. A moment later, he emerged with a little plastic first-aid case she'd seen in supermarkets. He put it on the couch next to her and opened it up. He prepared a small bandage with ointment and wrapped it around a cut that went over the ball of her foot and up behind her big toe.

He moved toward Shelly and then took a step back when Shelly recoiled. "Would you rather do hers?"

"That would probably be a good idea." Natalie shifted to face Shelly. "Can I see where you got the cut running?" When Shelly lifted her leg into Natalie's lap, she pulled off the slipper and used Rick's supplies to clean and bandage the wound in the arch of Shelly's foot.

"Ouch." Shelly's soft moan was barely audible. She had to be exhausted by now. When Natalie finished, Shelly leaned into the throw pillows in the corner of the sofa.

As Natalie balled up the wrappers and put everything back into the first-aid kit, she asked, "How did you learn to fight like that?"

"I was in the Special Forces."

Natalie waited but he didn't elaborate. She didn't feel comfortable pushing for more. They didn't know each other.

"If you don't mind me asking, what were you doing outside at this hour?" It was a fair question. She imagined most people were asleep in their beds during the hours Natalie often found herself outside needing fresh air.

"I—I don't sleep well. Sometimes I go outside when I wake from…for the cool air." She didn't want to get into her personal details with a stranger. Especially one that was looking at her with suspicion, as though she might be involved in something that would create this situation.

He nodded toward Shelly. "You said she saw a woman

being drowned in the river. Do you know who the woman was?"

"No." She turned to Shelly to ask her, but she was curled into the corner of the couch, dozing off. Natalie lowered her voice. "I think she would have told me if she recognized the woman. It's not likely. We don't know anyone here."

"How long have you lived here?" He kept his voice low.

"We don't actually live here. We came six months ago. It's temporary."

Rick's expression tensed again. "Are you okay? I mean other than what happened tonight?"

She wanted to spill it all out, but how could she? Rick had done a lot for them tonight but he was a stranger. He wouldn't want to hear about all of the heartache she had endured in the weeks leading up to coming to Maple Rapids. It had been so impulsive. And very unlike her.

He was watching her. Waiting for an answer. How much did she want to share? Was there a way to tell him enough without sharing too much? Then she began to wonder where the police were. Why hadn't they come yet? Surely, the things Rick told them would warrant a fast response. Unless he hadn't actually called the police. If not, then whom did she hear on the phone? It wasn't a 911 operator. It sounded as though he'd called the police station directly. But it really could have been anyone.

Rick watched a range of emotions pass over Natalie's face. He was beginning to worry what else was going on with her. Then she shifted off the couch. He reached out to help and she hesitated before she took his arm for support. He helped her over to the island in the kitchen and onto a stool.

"I want to let her sleep. She must be exhausted." She seemed to be avoiding the question he'd asked. That only made him worry more. But he'd let it go for now. He wasn't sure how much he actually wanted to know. He'd been very careful about getting involved with people in the last four years. And this situation could go south very easily. He wouldn't desert them but he wasn't keen on putting himself in a position to be responsible for anyone. He couldn't stand it if he lost them. Once the police arrived, he'd let them take over.

"When do you think the police will get here?" She seemed just as eager for their arrival as he was.

Rick went around to the other side of the island so he could face her and give her a little space. She seemed uncomfortable with him. He couldn't blame her, after someone had chased her through the woods earlier. "I'm not sure. They don't exactly move fast around here. Nothing like this ever happens. And Ed, the dispatcher, said something else was going on. If they don't show up soon, I'll call again." He watched her nodding, her eyes full of something he wasn't sure how to read. "Can I get you a drink or something?" He pulled open the refrigerator and took out two bottles of water. He put them on the counter in front of her.

"Thank you. I'll have some in a little while." She definitely didn't trust him.

Rick stood watching her, trying to get a sense of what she might be caught up in. She didn't seem the type but this could easily be a bad situation she'd gotten herself into. Then he realized she probably wouldn't want the cops involved if she was a criminal. He had to stop trying to find the dark side of every new person he met. Not that he could rule out the possibility that Natalie had done something to put herself in this situation. Either way, he couldn't help if he had no idea what he was actually dealing with. "Can you tell me why you were down by the river to begin with? What brought you outside? Did you hear something?" He tried to keep his tone neutral, hoping she might open up.

"I have nightmares. I go outside because I need to cool down. There was a fire. Shelly's parents died. I had been staying with them after a breakup. My brother... I can imagine the things you must be thinking. So I'll just tell you." It was as if she'd read his thoughts. "I brought my niece here for a change of scenery. I've been homeschooling her for the last six months. She wants to go back home. Back to her friends and school. We're from Spring Lake. In New Jersey. I should have left a while ago. I wish I had now." Her lips quivered for a moment and then she sucked in a quick breath and steadied herself. "I just needed a little more time. I'll take her home now..." She paused. "I'm sorry I spilled that all out that way. You just seemed to be looking at me like—like I might be the criminal. I figured I'd better explain."

Rick was surprised how well she seemed to have read his thoughts. It was unusual. Most people found him very difficult to figure out. It kind of impressed him. He also felt regret for making her feel that way and for doubting her.

"I'm so sorry for your loss. That must have been difficult."

Natalie nodded slightly. "It's just me and Shelly now. We're all that's left of our family. Sometimes I'm not sure I'll be enough for her."

"I find that hard to believe. She seems to trust you." That wasn't what he wanted to say. "What I mean is, it's

Addie Ellis 27

obvious you put her first. It couldn't have been easy to carry her with your foot in that condition."

Before he could say more, there was a knock at the door. He looked through the window and saw a police car parked out front. He should have pulled the curtains closed. He wasn't usually that careless. If the masked man had come back, he would have had a clear shot at them through the bare glass.

He walked over to the door and, just to be sure, he asked, "Who's there?"

"It's Pete Dennis." Rick recognized his old friend's voice and pulled the door open. Pete came inside with Todd Murphy close behind. He was a younger officer. Maybe mid-twenties, with a mop of brown hair and light blue eyes.

Pete's slate-blue eyes swept the room and landed on Natalie and then Shelly. He seemed to take note of the bandages on their feet and the scratches on their arms and legs. He was a sturdy man in his early thirties with dark hair and a serious demeanor. "Wanna tell me what happened here tonight?"

Rick moved next to Natalie. "I'll let her tell you what took place before they got here. A man wearing a ski mask was chasing them when I came out after hearing one of them scream. He proceeded to attack me trying to get to them. And he made an effort to disguise his voice. He wanted me to stay out of it. The whole thing was strange. You hear anything like this going on around town, Pete?"

Pete shook his head. "Can't say that I have. But... Well, let me hear what she has to say." He focused on Natalie. "How about we start with your name."

Todd was taking notes as they spoke.

"I'm Natalie Owens." She told him where her cottage

was. Rick was familiar with it. He'd been to many of them in that part of town as a kid. She told Pete pretty much the same thing she'd told him, without the part about the nightmares or the loss of family. Then Rick realized he didn't know what had happened with the breakup she'd mentioned that made her stay with her brother. It occurred to him that her niece may not have survived if she hadn't been there. It seemed likely that Natalie had been the one to get her out of the house.

Todd spoke up, bringing Rick back to the conversation. "Anyone with him?"

Rick shook his head. "Not that I saw."

Both officers turned to Natalie. She shook her head. "I didn't see anyone else. Shelly saw the woman she thought was me, but I have no idea what may or may not have actually happened down by the river."

A look passed between Pete and Todd. It made Rick uneasy.

"What's up?" Rick was eager to find out what they weren't saying.

Shelly sat up and looked around. Natalie got off the stool and Rick quickly moved to her side to help her back over to the sofa, where she sat down and put her arm around her niece. Then she looked at Pete. "What were you about to tell us?"

"The reason it took us a little longer to get up here is because there's a woman missing. Her sister reported it a few hours ago." He looked at Shelly. "Can you tell me what the woman you saw looked like?"

Shelly looked up at Natalie and when she nodded for the little girl to share what she knew, she turned back to Pete and spoke very clearly. "She had dark hair. She looked like Aunt Natty from behind but not from the front."

Pete's expression hardened. Rick asked, "Who is missing?"

"Angela Baker." Pete's voice was strained. Rick knew he was pretty friendly with a lot of the people in town. He'd grown up with most of them. And Angela could easily pass for Natalie from behind. She wasn't nearly as pretty but they had a similar build and hair style.

Rick looked over at Natalie and Shelly sitting together. They looked so much alike. He would have believed they were mother and daughter. They both had big brown eyes and a thick mane of dark curly hair. They were both slim and very pretty. The woman's face had more refined features and the little girl's had softer lines. They both looked so vulnerable. Who would do something like this? At least they would be safe now that Pete was involved.

Seeming to sense the tension building in the room, Natalie pulled Shelly closer to her. Then it suddenly felt as though everything was exploding around them. Glass was flying through the air as the sound of rapid gunfire ripped through the quiet room.

Natalie pulled Shelly to the floor, covering the child with her own body, and tried to shuffle away from the glass shards flying in every direction. Away from the violence that had suddenly erupted all around them. Todd dropped to the floor and Pete had gone into the small hallway between the bedrooms to take cover as the bullets sprayed across the wall and tore open the plaid sofa that had been in this cabin since Rick was a child. Then everything abruptly fell into silence, except for the rain and wind pushing through the broken windows. Rick looked up, realizing he had thrown himself over the woman and child he barely knew, then gazed around and tried to figure out who in the room had survived and who might be dead.

THREE

Rick eased off Natalie when he felt her moving beneath him and checked that she and Shelly hadn't been hit. There was glass everywhere and Todd Murphy was flat on his back, bleeding from his side. His hand was pressing into the wound but it didn't stop the blood that was spilling onto the floor. Rick scanned the room, searching for Pete Dennis, hoping he avoided the barrage of bullets that made his peaceful little cabin look like a war zone. Pete was still tucked between the bedrooms. He took the radio strapped to his shoulder and called for backup. He sounded calm but was clear about the urgency.

Rick cautiously got into a crouching position. Natalie was looking around, her eyes wide. He couldn't imagine what this must have been like for her and the little girl. They couldn't possibly be accustomed to situations like this. They hadn't gone through the training he had. They hadn't been taught to see beyond the fear and horror to complete an objective like he had. If he wasn't worried for their safety, he'd have already run out the door to hunt the gunmen down. It would have been instinct. But this feeling, this fear of failing anyone else kept him from leaving before he was sure Pete could take over. After what happened to his unit he was eager to remove himself from the equation. The confusion in Shelly's eyes was enough to make him want to be done with this whole situation. He was beginning to care in the exact way he'd wanted to avoid. He couldn't be sure of the outcome and wouldn't allow himself to let this become personal. But he would do what he could in the moment. Rick would help out until they were out of his cabin. Then he'd head back home and see what he could do to freshen up the training program he'd created.

After leaving the service, Rick found that many of the things he'd learned could be applied to corporate environments in ways he never would've imagined when he was still serving. He ended up developing a corporate training program that companies could use to teach employees how to communicate more effectively, build confidence, learn sensitivity and appropriate workplace behaviors, and how to take steps to move into leadership positions. It had felt like the perfect fit for a while. It tapped into things he'd learned as a soldier and gave him a sense of purpose. But lately, it hadn't been as fulfilling. Once the programs were in place and required very little from him to sell them to businesses, he was once again left with a lot of time to overthink the decisions he'd made that led to him ending his career as a Special Forces officer. The one benefit that still remained was that he could work remotely from anywhere with internet access. He was grateful for the flexibility while he tried to figure out what he was meant to do next. And where that would be.

In the present situation, Rick needed to make sure Natalie and Shelly weren't injured. He tried to get Natalie's attention. "Hey, are you okay?"

Her eyes were darting around the room. "We're fine but I think he needs help," she replied, pointing toward

Todd. She shuffled across the floor on her hands and knees, careful to avoid the broken glass, grabbed a dish towel from the counter and then crawled over to Todd. She pressed the towel against his bullet wound and looked up at Rick. He was about to join her when he felt Shelly burrow into his side. He put his arm around her, trying to provide some comfort, and looked at her aunt. Natalie's eyes welled up with tears at the sight of them. He could see she was torn between helping Todd and comforting her niece. Looking at them, he couldn't help but wonder who would want to kill them so desperately that they would shoot up his cabin with police inside?

Pete came back into the room and when he saw Todd, he dropped to his knees and took over for Natalie. He grabbed the radio strapped to his shoulder. "I need paramedics up here. We have an officer down. Repeat. We have an officer down. Gunshot wound to the side. A lot of blood loss." He leaned down to his partner. "Hang in there. Help is on the way."

When Shelly started to cry, Natalie moved quickly to get to her. Once she had the little girl in her arms, Rick grabbed the gun he kept strapped underneath the couch and moved toward the back door. He couldn't risk the possibility of another assault on the cabin. He wouldn't be able to live with it if something happened to them. He looked at Natalie before he went out the door. "Stay down until I get back." When she nodded, he slipped out.

He figured that the gunman had either run out of bullets and taken off, or he was waiting outside getting ready to strike again. Since he shot from the front, Rick went out the back. He pressed himself against the outer wall of the cabin and took a quick look around the corner. The rain quickly soaked his already damp hair and clothes. The downpour was cold and heavy, pushing a chill through his body. He'd been trained to ignore just about any kind of weather, but it had been some time since he'd been in a situation like this. Still, it wasn't difficult to tune out the water flowing into his eyes and streaming down his face and neck. Or the way the saturated ground wrapped around his feet like wet sponges. Rick's focus was on the sounds around him and the search for any hint of movement as he scanned every tree and dark shadow within striking distance of the cabin.

When he didn't see anything, he hurried to the front corner and peered around from the side. He continued to listen for movement, his ears separating the sound of the rain from the forest itself. He watched the nearby trees for any sign of shifting branches. The instincts he had refined during his time with the army seemed to drop right back into place. As though no time had passed. When it became clear that there was no one out there, he went back inside through the front door.

"I think he's gone. At least for now. He probably emptied his magazine and took off."

Pete was still holding the blood-soaked rag against his partner's wound. He looked up at Rick. "Once the paramedics come and take Todd to the hospital, I'll need the three of you to come down to the station to tell me everything you saw and anything you can remember about the shooter. I'm sure I'll have some more questions by then, too."

Rick nodded. "Of course." He considered the events that had just unfolded. "I think they'll need protective custody," he said, nodding toward Natalie and the child. "I have a feeling this guy isn't going to give up."

Pete was nodding as he spoke. "We'll talk about that."

Rick wiped the mud and moisture from his feet and put on a pair of shoes. It was impossible to sit still and wait. Instead, he started pacing the room, checking the windows and doors. He tried to listen through the storm for any movement outside. Not an easy task with how heavy the rain had become. It was as though rocks were bouncing off the roof instead of water. It didn't help when the wind kicked up and pushed a cold mist through the broken window.

It wasn't long before the paramedics and several police officers arrived. The flurry of activity was a reminder of things he'd seen before. This wasn't nearly as bad. Todd Murphy was probably going to be alright. If the bullet had hit just a little differently, he might not have survived. It was another reminder of how quickly things can change. How easy it was to lose people.

He watched one of the paramedics check Natalie and Shelly. It could have been them. What if he hadn't been here? He had been thinking about leaving for days. The thought of it had him on edge. His parents would have gotten a call about a woman and child murdered outside their cabin. Maybe they wouldn't have even told him. Or worse, the masked man might have taken the bodies away and no one would have ever known what happened to them. Rick shook his head, trying to push away the muddled thoughts. It was sometimes like a runaway train once his mind started rolling. It had been this way since he got back. He had tried therapy but it hadn't been the right fit.

Trying to calm the frenzy of possible outcomes flashing across his mind, Rick focused on the way Shelly was wrapped around Natalie, her face buried in her aunt's neck. At least he had been useful tonight. The question was whether the police were truly equipped to take over.

They had never dealt with anything like this in Maple Rapids before. He knew Pete wouldn't expect him to do anything more. As much as he wanted to be done with it, the idea of walking away was gnawing at him. Natalie was clearly shaken and Pete's focus was consumed by getting Todd medical attention and directing the others in the tasks of their investigation. It left her and Shelly vulnerable. He stepped closer to Natalie.

"How about if we wait in the bedroom so she can lie down for a little while?" He nodded toward Shelly.

Natalie had that vacant look again. Rick had an idea of how that felt. How becoming numb helped shield a person from the enormity of what was happening. She followed him without a word, carrying her niece on her hip as she limped along. Rick closed the door and made sure the curtains covered the windows. He kept the light off in case the shooter came back. No point in giving him another target. Not that Rick believed the masked man would return with so many cops wandering around.

Natalie sat on the edge of the bed and laid Shelly down. She crawled up toward the pillows and curled under the blanket. The poor little girl was so exhausted from everything that had happened that she fell asleep a moment after her head hit the pillow. He noticed that someone had given Natalie little white paper booties to wear. It wasn't much, but at least it was something.

Rick spoke just above a whisper to keep from waking Shelly. "We can stay in here until we leave." When Natalie nodded, he sat on the edge of the bed and angled his body toward her. "Did you remember anything else? Anything that might help?"

Natalie shook her head. "I never saw his face. And I didn't see the woman. There was something in the way he moved, though. Like he would have done anything to get to us. Do you know what I mean?"

"I think so. I saw it in his eyes. He was determined. I've seen it before. That darkness. People like that don't have remorse. They only care about their objective, regardless of who they have to hurt." Rick hadn't only seen it with the enemy. He had seen it with men he'd served with. He tried to keep them out of missions he worked. He preferred people he could trust to think on their feet and make quick decisions as things evolved.

"Did he talk to you?" Rick thought about the strange growl the masked man had spoken with. And the way he'd stared at Rick. As if he had been trying to communicate something. The familiarity of his eyes was still bugging him.

"No. He didn't say anything. I wonder if that woman Shelly saw was the missing person the officer mentioned." She got quiet again. Then said, "I should have taken her back to my house months ago. She's been asking to go. It's my fault Shelly had to go through this. I'm not cut out to take care of her. She could have died tonight..." Natalie's voice trailed off.

Rick shifted a little closer. "Don't think that way. There's no way you could have known this would happen. You can't blame yourself." He turned toward the sleeping child. "Look at her. She's safe because of you. You fought for her. You didn't hesitate to throw yourself over her when that maniac opened fire. Not everyone would have reacted that way."

Before he could say more, the bedroom door opened, letting dim light pour into the room. Pete Dennis had blood from his partner down the front of his shirt and on the cuffs of his sleeves. He gave a quick nod of his head toward the activity outside the bedroom.

"I have a few things to wrap up here and then we'll leave for the station. I'll take your statements there while everything's fresh. Some techs will be here for a bit collecting evidence. Besides, you shouldn't stay here in case the shooter comes back once everyone clears out."

Rick stood up. "I'll bring them in my truck. They'll be more comfortable than they would be in the back of a police car." He watched Natalie for a reaction. She turned to Pete and waited. Was she uncomfortable with the idea of riding with Rick? He was only trying to make the ride less stressful since he also had to go to the station to give his account of the night's events.

"I guess that would be alright. But we stay together on the road." Pete started toward the door once Rick nodded, then stopped and glanced back at them. "I'm trying to get a better understanding of what happened tonight. Miss Owens, can you tell me what brings you and your niece to Maple Rapids? Are her parents with you?"

Natalie's eyes glazed over. As though the questions were somehow physically painful. She stared at the floor before finally meeting Pete's stern gaze. Did he suspect her of being involved? Rick had considered it but he was beginning to rethink that possibility.

"It's just the two of us. Shelly's parents... My brother... and his wife died six months ago. I'm her legal guardian." She paused for a long moment, as though saying those words had drained her. Pete opened his mouth to say something and stopped when she continued. "We came here six months ago to—to get a change of scenery. I... We don't really know anyone here. I don't know who was in the river or who that man was." She glanced back at

Shelly, who was still sound asleep. Then she turned back to Pete. Rick couldn't be sure with the light in the room being so dim but Natalie seemed to be shrinking into herself. The way her shoulders slumped made him want to put his arms around her and hold her up. Knowing what she and Shelly had lost made the events of the night seem so much worse. He looked at the little girl curled under the covers in his bed and realized that she and her aunt might be the first people he had come across in the last four years that might have an inkling of what he had been feeling. But to lose both of her parents at such a young age was a different kind of sorrow than what Rick had been grappling with.

Pete seemed to pick up on Natalie's state of mind and softened his tone. "I'm sorry for your loss." Natalie nodded, her expression a mix of emotions in the light that slipped through as Pete pushed the door open a little further. Then he stepped closer. "Is there anything else you can remember about your interaction with him?"

"He knows Shelly was there when he was pushing that woman under the water." Her tone was low and laced with worry. "She said he saw her. That he looked angry that she was there. Those were her words. Now, all of this. I don't think he'll stop until..." Her voice caught on the last few words.

Pete nodded. "How did she come to see him? What I mean is, why were the two of you out there so late?"

"I told you all of this earlier."

"Humor me. Tell me again. You might remember something new."

Natalie took a breath and obliged Pete's request. "She saw the woman walking through the yard. She followed, thinking it was me. I woke from a bad dream and needed some air. The nightmares... Shelly knows I go outside at night sometimes. I heard a commotion by the river and went down to see, expecting to find some teenagers messing around. I never expected... Shelly came running before I could get down there to see anything. I followed and then tried to get her away from the man she saw. We ended up here. You know the rest."

Pete must have decided to let the rest of the questions wait until they went to the police station. "We'll head out in a few minutes. They already took Todd to the hospital." Then he walked out, leaving the door open.

Natalie stood up and limped around the side of the bed to get Shelly. He wasn't sure if she had been hurt anywhere other than her foot. He had given her some space when one of the paramedics checked her out. What he really wondered about now was her mention of nightmares. How bad were they that she needed to go outside? And what was it about the night of the fire that was haunting her enough to make her want to leave her hometown?

"I can get her if you want. You look like you're in pain." He suppressed an urge to hold her up. To provide some kind of support. She seemed a little closed-off now. Not as open as she had been before Pete came in. There was a tension in her movements.

Natalie tilted her head in his direction, her eyes unreadable in the darkness on that side of the bed. Even with more light flowing through the open door, the shadow over her face kept her features from view. Then she nodded and stepped back. Her voice was soft. "Thank you. For everything. You saved our lives tonight."

"You needn't thank me for anything." Rick came around the side of the bed and lifted Shelly into his arms. Her damp brown curls fell over his shoulder as she nuzzled against him. Something about holding this little girl brought emotions to the surface that had been locked away for a long time. They didn't deserve any more heartache.

On the way out, he grabbed a bag of essentials he kept at the ready. An old habit from his time in the service. He was always prepared to run. Always ready for something to go wrong. Another one of those things he had come here to work on. Not that tonight wouldn't perpetuate his necessity to keep vigilant. He wondered when it would be safe to come back to his family cabin again. If he would even be around by then.

Rick carried Shelly, with Natalie next to him, out to his pickup truck. Pete was by Natalie's other side and two officers followed behind them. The rain was still steady, the sky a black sheet, making it difficult to see anything around them. As they approached the truck, the sound of cracking branches froze them all in place. Rick listened carefully. Small sticks snapped beyond the tree line in his backyard. Pete and the other two officers pulled out their weapons and seemed to be listening and watching for where the noises were coming from.

Hazel Clarke, one of the officers who had arrived with the paramedics, took cover on the side of his truck bed and aimed her gun toward the trees, keeping her head low. She was new to the force and young, around twenty-five years old. Rick had spoken to her a few times at the diner with Pete. Her mother had named her for the hazel color of her eyes. Her dirty blond hair was pulled back in a ponytail. She had a small frame with a slim build, but didn't seem to have an ounce of fear. Rick opened the back door of the truck and got Natalie and Shelly to stay low on the floor. He threw his duffel on the seat and closed the door as quietly as possible. Then he pulled his own gun and stood next to Hazel.

They waited, listening to the rhythm of the water tapping down on every surface around them. It was deafening, the silence woven between the pattering of the rain. Then a large snap brought his gun around to another part of the trees. A dark shadow emerged from the foliage. He aimed at what appeared to be center mass, his finger loose on the trigger.

"Stop and identify yourself!" Pete called out with the kind of authority he rarely needed to use.

Rick's finger tightened a little as the figure stopped for a moment and then started walking forward again. Was it the same man? The pouring rain and lack of light made it nearly impossible to see at this distance. Pete called out again and then the dark figure started walking faster. The officers were all yelling out at once but the person kept moving. Rick settled into position, his breathing steady, and took aim. Everything else melted away. He began to put the slightest bit of pressure on the trigger as he focused, waiting to be sure.

Pete and the other officers were calling out but the person kept moving. Rick watched the arms for any shift. For any hint that they might be raising a weapon. Then the person's arms came up into the air. Rick tried to see through the darkness. Through the sheets of water. The person stopped walking and two of the officers cautiously started walking into the yard. Was this a trick? A way to separate them to make them easier to pick off? He kept his breathing steady, his eyes trained on the target. He had to make sure no one else got shot. He couldn't fail them.

FOUR

Natalie heard all of the commotion outside, sending a frenzy of panic through her body. She held Shelly beneath her, pushed low between the front and rear seats. She could hear a woman's voice suddenly yelling from a distance. The rain pounding against the metal body of the truck made it difficult to understand at first. Then it became clear.

"Don't shoot! It's me, Angela."

Natalie heard a male officer's voice. It was deep and calm and filled with warning. "Stop where you are. Keep your hands up where we can see them. Don't move."

Natalie dared to peek through the rear window. She could see the dark outline of a woman in the yard. Shelly tried to sit up but Natalie gently pushed her back down.

Officer Pete Dennis took a step forward. "Lower your weapons. It's Angela. The missing woman. Angela Baker." Then he turned to the woman. "Angela? What are you doing out here? Where have you been? Everyone's been out looking for you." Pete seemed to know her personally.

"I was out for a hike. My ankle twisted in a dip in the path. I didn't see it under the leaves. I fell and hit my head. I'm not sure how long I was out. It was dark and raining when I woke up. I got so turned around. I've been wandering for a while. I'm a little dizzy." She walked over to Officer Dennis. Rick shifted in front of the back door of the truck, where he had pushed Natalie and Shelly through a few moments before. She watched the exchange between the woman and the officer. Pete Dennis looked relieved to see her. He told the woman he would give her a ride to the hospital. The woman reluctantly agreed and let him put her in the front seat of his police car. Then he came over to Rick.

"Meet me at the station. I need to get her checked out. I can see some blood on the back of her head." Rick nodded and immediately went around to the driver's side and got in.

Natalie was about to get onto the seat with Shelly when Rick spoke in a soft tone. "Stay low until we get out of the woods. That guy could still be out there. Let's not give him a clear target."

"What about you?" Natalie worried that the masked man might take a shot at him, even if he believed Rick was alone, for helping them.

"He's not interested in me." Rick started driving down the rough road. She wondered how he could be sure of that. Why he didn't seem to have any fear of getting hurt. They all remained quiet, the uncertainty of where the masked man could be keeping them on high alert. There was nothing to see through the windows but darkness and water streaming down the glass. At least it was warm. Their wet clothes would have been harder to endure if it had been one of those chillier nights. It wasn't uncommon being so close to the river. When the dirt turned to pavement, Rick finally broke the silence. "I think you can sit up now."

Addie Ellis

Tension filled the truck as they traversed the dark wet roads. The sound of the windshield wipers scraped against what was left of Natalie's nerves. She closed her eyes as she tried to pray. She hardly knew where to begin. She prayed that the woman in the river had somehow survived. That Shelly would overcome the violence they had endured. There was an officer on his way to the hospital, and that poor woman from the woods may have a head injury. She couldn't form anything coherent, other than a stream of anxious thoughts. Still, Natalie believed that the Lord would understand what she was trying to convey.

When they arrived at the police station, they hurried to get inside. The rain had become heavier and the wind had picked up, beginning to snap tree branches. They ran, trying to avoid the wide puddles along the sidewalk. The little white booties she had been given were getting soaked and falling apart. When they stepped through the double glass doors, a policeman brought them to an office and offered them a seat on a large tan leather couch. Natalie sat with Shelly. Rick paced and seemed to be keeping watch. He walked the room in a pattern, checking the windows and the door on a loop. His handsome features were tense. He looked so focused, as if he had done things like this before. The wet clothes clinging to his muscular build didn't seem to bother him. Natalie wondered what kinds of things he had done in his time as a soldier to prepare him so well to engage with a killer without an ounce of fear.

Officer Dennis came in and wanted to go over everything that had happened. He remained standing as he dove right into the questions. Rick asked about Todd Murphy, but Officer Dennis wanted to get as many details as they could remember first. He was most interested in what

Shelly had seen because the killer had put on a mask before Natalie or Rick had the chance to see his face. Natalie couldn't tell him much other than that the assailant was average height and he looked sturdily built. Rick confirmed it, explaining that the masked man had been very strong and seemed to really know how to handle himself. Rick gave some details that made Natalie aware that the masked man was even more dangerous than she had realized. It was also clear that Rick's background had given him experience with dangerous people. It was the way he described what happened. There was no hesitation or fear. He was clear and concise.

When Officer Dennis turned to Shelly, she buried her face into Natalie's chest. Natalie rubbed her back and spoke in a gentle tone. "Is there anything else you can remember about what that man looked like? It might help the police find him."

Shelly glanced up at the officer. Her voice was soft, laden with fear. "He looked angry when he saw me. His hair was short... He was hurting that woman... He tried to catch us."

Officer Dennis gave her some time, then asked, "Can you tell me anything else about him? Did he look old? Young? Did you see the color of his eyes? His hair?"

Shelly shrugged. She took a moment, looking around as she appeared to be pulling something from her memory. "His eyes were dark. He wasn't old like a grandpa, but older than Aunt Natty. He had black clothes. His hair was dark, like yours." She stopped for a moment. "He made the lady scream. He was hurting her. She asked him to stop a bunch of times." Then she leaned her head on Natalie's shoulder. "I think she knew him." This gave a bit of a wide range. Natalie was twenty-seven. The killer could be anywhere from his mid-thirties to somewhere in his fifties based on that description. The possibility that the victim knew her attacker seemed to cause an uneasy shift in the officer's demeanor. He took a step back as he seemed to retreat into himself, deep in thought.

Then he turned back to Shelly. "What about the woman? You said she looked like your aunt from the back. Can you tell me anything else about her? Was she tall? Short? Did you get a good look at her face?"

Shelly sat up again. "She was older, like the man. She was kicking and punching him when he dragged her into the river." When Officer Dennis didn't ask anything more, she leaned back into Natalie's arms.

It was time to go back to Spring Lake. This had been the last thing Natalie had anticipated when she'd brought Shelly here six months ago. They had stayed too long. She wondered if the police would let them leave now that Shelly was the only one to have seen the killer's face. The turmoil of the last few hours made her long for the comfort of the home she thought she didn't want anymore. She missed the friends she'd left behind to clear her head in the mountains. She hoped her teaching job was still being held for her and tried to imagine what she would do if it wasn't. The one thing she was sure of was that she didn't want to be in Maple Rapids anymore.

Officer Dennis moved a little closer. "Do you think you would recognize the man and the woman if you saw either of them again?" When Shelly nodded, he said, "You're doing a great job." He was being kind. She hadn't really given him much, but Natalie thought she'd done well under the circumstances. She had always been a tenacious little girl. "Can you tell me why you were by the river?"

Shelly looked up at Natalie with tears filling her eyes

again. This was too much. Natalie turned to the officer. "I think she needs a break. And I've already told you why she was out there. I've told you everything multiple times now."

Officer Dennis nodded and sat down behind his desk. He proceeded to ask basic questions that Natalie could answer, jotting it all down for his report. He made note of their full names and the address of the cottage where they were staying. He didn't have to ask Rick. The officer already seemed to know all of his information. When he finished, he made a call to the hospital for an update. While he was on the phone, Natalie asked Shelly why she had been outside. Why she had left the cottage without telling her.

Shelly whispered her answer. "I saw the lady. I thought it was you. I wanted to see where you were going."

"That was the only reason? You weren't out there already? It's okay if you were. I need you to tell me the truth. Were you already down by the water when the man and the woman showed up?" Natalie waited, unsure what the answer would be. She knew Shelly had been growing restless. That she wanted to go back to Spring Lake. But to sneak out in the middle of the night? It didn't seem like something Shelly would do.

Shelly shook her head. "I didn't go out until I saw her." Her voice got softer. "I wanted to go with you. Am I in trouble for going outside without permission?" Shelly looked at her with those big pleading eyes. That adorable face she made when she got caught doing something she shouldn't.

Natalie noticed Rick watching them as she pulled Shelly into a tight embrace. "No. You're not in trouble.

You were so brave. I'm just so happy you're safe now. But please don't go outside without me again, okay?"

Shelly nodded and looked at Officer Dennis as he hung up the phone. He had news about Todd Murphy, the officer who had been shot in Rick's cabin.

"He's out of surgery and stable. They're optimistic that he'll make a full recovery. He'll be laid up for a couple weeks but the bullet didn't cause any serious damage." He focused on Natalie. "I think it would be best if officers stay outside your home until we find this guy." He paused for a moment, seeming to consider something. "We haven't found the woman Shelly saw yet. Given the weather tonight, it's possible she was pulled out of the area by the current." His eyes seemed to search his desk. "It's also possible that she's wounded somewhere, waiting for help. We have people out looking but there's a lot of ground to cover. For now, I think we should get you both home."

"What about that woman? The one that had been missing? Did you get any news about her condition?" Natalie hoped she was alright.

Officer Dennis nodded. "She's fine. They'll be sending her home soon."

Rick stepped away from the window. He had been watching diligently the whole time they sat in that office. "Maybe I should stay with them until we can be sure they're safe." There was a kind of strain to his tone. As though the offer might be difficult for him.

A look passed between them, then Officer Dennis focused his gaze on Natalie.

She wasn't sure what to say. Did she want Rick in her house? She barely knew him. And he had already done so much for them. Was it fair to expect more? She looked at the officer, trying to keep from meeting Rick's eyes. "Is that necessary? Do you think this guy would know who we are or where we live? There are at least fifteen to twenty other cottages along that road. They all back to the river. And we went in a completely different direction when we ran." She thought about the way he had trailed them through the woods. She had been worried about going to the cottage because of how close it was to where Shelly saw him, but he couldn't have had time to go there and look for them and then catch up so quickly. Still, it was impossible to be sure what that man knew.

"I doubt it. It's more of a precaution. He followed you to Rick's cabin. There's no reason to believe he knows where you live. You said you heard him gaining on you as you ran in a different direction. I don't see how he would know you didn't live with Rick. As a precaution, I'll have officers go and check your place before we take you home. Assuming everything is still secure, I think a couple uniforms out front would be sufficient." Officer Dennis's phone rang. He reached for it and then glanced back at Natalie. "If you go out to reception I'll have someone bring you home shortly. I'll come by in a few hours to check on things. Please let me know if you or Shelly remember anything else." Then he took the call.

Natalie and Shelly walked out into the reception area with Rick following behind them. There was a counter and a man sitting at a desk typing on his computer. The sun was coming up, sending warm light through the glass doors. At least the rain had finally stopped. Natalie wished she could stop her feelings of guilt as well. She should have taken her niece back to Spring Lake. She would now. But Shelly would need some sleep before they got on the road, and Natalie wanted to pack some things to take with them, too. She would mention her plan to Pete when he came by later.

They stood beside the counter for what felt like a long time before Rick spoke to her. He had been quiet as they waited for the police to take them home. Her feet were cold after being barefoot in the rain most of the night. At least their hair and clothes were nearly dry.

"You look tired. You should sit." He gestured toward a row of chairs to one side of the counter, against a wall.

Natalie sat and Shelly climbed into the chair next to her and rested her head in Natalie's lap. They were both exhausted. Rick took the seat on her other side and angled toward her, facing the glass doors. She wanted to ask him so many questions but didn't want to be intrusive. Yet, her mouth started moving, against her better judgment. It must have been the exhaustion.

"You seem to be pretty adept at…defending yourself. How did you…? What did you do when you were in the army? Did you have to do things like that a lot?" Something shifted in his eyes and she immediately regretted asking.

He inhaled a deep breath and started talking as he let it out. "I had extensive training. And I had a lot of…practical experience. I haven't done anything like that in four years. It's not something I take any pleasure in. It's more of a way to protect myself or help others when they aren't able to protect themselves."

Unexpected relief eased some of her tension. After seeing what he was capable of, it was impossible not to wonder if he was one of those men who sought out danger to have an excuse to use his skills. "You don't like to fight?"

His face hardened a little. Then he shook his head. "There were times when I was forced to defend myself and others. It's not something I like to do, but when it's necessary, I don't hesitate. It's kind of like being on autopilot. My body just seems to know what to do."

Natalie could understand that. Something similar had taken over her body the night of the fire. There hadn't been any time to think. The flames had moved very quickly and she had somehow done things she never would have thought possible before that evening. It was as though she had suddenly become faster and stronger. And fear hadn't been able to stop her. She couldn't help but wonder if he felt any of that kind of fear. He seemed so calm. Steady. As though he could take on anything he faced. It was rather impressive.

"Are you sure you don't want me to come along? I don't mind." Rick's tired green eyes were filled with an anguish that hadn't been there before. Not when she ran toward his cabin. Not when he faced off with a killer. She wasn't sure what to make of it. He barely knew them. Did he feel obligated to keep helping them? He was clearly brave and very kind to be willing to protect them the way he had, but he couldn't be this worried for strangers, could he? She considered letting him come, in spite of what she knew was right. Though it wasn't fair to ask any more of him, as much as she wanted to. He wasn't a police officer. He wasn't family or even a friend. There was no reason for him to feel obligated to help them. Other than the fact that he was the kind of man who would put his own life at risk for strangers. She didn't want to take advantage of his kindness. And she didn't want something to happen to him after everything he'd done. He was clearly in need of sleep.

"You've already done so much," she said finally. "Honestly, I think we're going to leave town later today. It's long past time."

Rick edged closer and looked like he was about to say something when two officers came in from outside. They both looked young with short hair and average builds. One of them addressed her.

"Miss Owens?" When she nodded, he continued. "We're going to take you home now. Your house has been cleared. If you would come this way?"

"Of course." Natalie rubbed her niece's back and woke her. They both stood up and she took Shelly's hand to leave. Then she stopped and turned back to Rick. "Thank you for everything. You could have turned us away. Closed the door and ignored what was happening. What you did...well, I will always be grateful." Then she went with the officers outside. Rick followed them through the doors and trailed them to the police cruiser.

As they walked along the sidewalk, avoiding what was left of the puddles, Shelly asked about breakfast. Natalie was too tired to explain why they couldn't go to the store to buy her favorite cereal. The pain throbbing through her toes along with the weariness making her sluggish made it difficult to think about much, other than getting far away from this place. Besides, she didn't imagine the police officers would want to drive them into the next town for a box of cereal. Natalie had found the shop over the bridge had more of the things she and Shelly needed than the store in Maple Rapids. They had gone there once when they had first arrived in the area and realized they needed to find a place with more of the things Shelly was used to. Natalie wanted to maintain some stability in her niece's life. As for right now, a box of cereal didn't seem important enough to go that far out of the way.

She told Shelly they'd see what they had when they got home. Once they were in the back seat of the police car, she looked out the window and saw Rick watching them pull away. She couldn't help but wonder if it had been a mistake not to let him come home with them.

Rick watched the black-and-white car drive away. He couldn't force Natalie to let him help. But it was difficult to stay out of it now. He felt responsible for them. He didn't want to fail them the way he had failed the people he had served with. It had been his mission. He was in charge. It didn't matter that no one blamed him. That there was no way to have foreseen the ambush. It had been an information-gathering assignment that had gone horribly wrong. They had split off into smaller groups, each having different roles to play. There wasn't supposed to be any interaction. But Rick had learned that no amount of planning guaranteed the outcome. The loss had been the end of his career. He couldn't continue. The medal he'd received for what he had done to rescue the few he'd managed to save was nothing more than a painful reminder of how he had failed the people who trusted him.

His insides tensed with the warring inside of him. As far as Natalie and her niece were concerned, he was off the hook. He could walk away. He had done his part. He'd kept them safe until the police took over. And Natalie didn't want his help. He was no longer responsible. It was Pete's job now. But Rick still felt like he should be there. He just couldn't figure out if it was his way of trying to make up for the men and women he had lost, or if there was something about this situation that was waking up that part of him that needed to protect the innocent.

The very thing that had motivated him to join the army twelve years ago.

If only Natalie had said yes.

He heard Shelly asking about one of those sugary kid's cereals he usually avoided. She seemed pretty disappointed when Natalie told her they didn't have it. He thought Arnie's store in town might carry it, or at least something similar. He had seen many like it in the grocery section. Maybe he could pick up a box and bring it to Natalie's house. It would give him an excuse to check on them. Before he could talk himself out of it, he got into his pickup truck and headed over to the store.

Arnie Standish had moved into town and bought the small general store about two years ago. He was probably in his late forties and walked with a limp that he'd had since Rick first met him. He was a pleasant man and had always kept an assortment of things in his store, including camping supplies, groceries and even a small selection of clothing. There wasn't a large variety of anything, but there was enough to take care of Rick's basic needs while staying in the cabin.

Rick was surprised by how many people were shopping this early. It was barely eight in the morning. There were a lot of familiar faces that he wasn't in the mood to talk to. He kept his head down as he hurried to the grocery aisle, where he searched for the right cereal box.

"Hey, Rick." He turned to see Dan Caraway. He was a sturdy man in his thirties who always took the time to say hello. Dan had been working for Arnie since he took over the store two years ago. "You're here early. What brings you into town this morning? Can I help you find anything?"

Rick picked up the box of cereal he had come for. At

least he thought it was the right one. They were all so colorful, now he wasn't quite sure. "Just picking up a few things."

"You don't usually go for the sugary stuff. Do you have some company?" Dan stood in front of him, eagerly awaiting an answer. "Someone with a kid?"

"Just trying something new, Dan. I'm in a rush, if you don't mind." Dan's endless questions didn't usually bother Rick, but today he didn't have the patience or the time.

"Oh, sure." Dan stepped aside. "We'll catch up later."

Rick tried to smile and then hurried to the register. He saw Dan walking over to straighten a shelf near the front of the store, where he spoke to a police officer who was asking questions about some hunting supplies. There were a few other men he recognized that walked over to the officer and tried to get the details about the events of the night before. The news had traveled faster than expected. It wasn't much of a surprise given the way gossip tended to spread in this little town. Those gossipers would all have plenty of questions for him once they realized he was involved.

Avoiding eye contact with pretty much everyone, he paid Arnie, took the cereal without a bag and hustled out to his truck. He would have to apologize for his curt behavior another time.

Once inside his truck, he realized that Natalie may not welcome the idea of him arriving unannounced. He drove slowly, taking the long way around, trying to figure out a way to explain showing up there. Maybe she wouldn't appreciate that he had been listening to her conversation with Shelly about breakfast. Or that he'd come after she told him not to. He pulled to the side of the road, trying to figure out if this was a good idea. If he even wanted to insert himself back into this situation now that the police had taken over. When his mind was made up, he pulled his truck back onto the road, praying he wasn't making the wrong decision.

FIVE

Last night had been one of the two scariest of Natalie's life. It was almost worse than the fire. That had all happened very fast. And she'd known that Shelly was safe the moment they had gotten outside the burning house. But last night... Being pursued by that man was terrifying and it felt like it would never end. Worse was the fear that their would-be attacker would return. How could he not when Shelly had seen his face? There was no way he would let her identify him.

After feeding Shelly and getting her to bed, Natalie took the opportunity for some much needed rest on the couch. She hadn't intended on dozing off, but the growing anxiety was adding to her exhaustion. As she was slipping into a dream about rafting down the river with her niece, she could feel her body beginning to drift away, that sense of knowing she was dreaming while a small part of her clutched to consciousness.

They had only tried rafting a few times since moving to the cottage. They enjoyed it but Natalie had been focusing on things that would help Shelly feel safe. The rough rapids sometimes made her niece fearful of falling in and being washed away in the current. After losing her parents in the fire, Shelly had been having a difficult time letting go of the fear that something bad might happen again. She sometimes came in to make sure Natalie was still there in the middle of the night. It explained why she had been so quick to run outside when she thought she saw Natalie walking into the woods. She was all Shelly had left.

A creaking noise drew Natalie's attention. The sound didn't fit. Not on the river. The groan of old wood floors woke her up from her dream. Natalie sat up and looked around. Had Pete come to check on them? She wasn't sure how much time had gone by. Maybe Shelly was awake.

Natalie eased off the couch and made her way slowly into the small hallway. That's when she came face-to-face with *him*. He still wore the black mask. His shoes weren't wet anymore. Oddly, she wondered if he had changed them. She stood frozen, trying to figure out how he'd gotten in here without the police in the cruiser out front seeing him. Taking a cautious step toward him, she peered into the bedroom. Shelly was still tucked under the covers sleeping. At least he hadn't gotten to her yet.

The question was whether to run screaming for the cops outside, or put herself between him and her niece. Either was a risk for different reasons. Running would leave him free to hurt Shelly if he didn't follow to stop her. Staying meant that he would get to Shelly once he dealt with Natalie. She took a tentative step backward. She was about to take another when he spoke.

"I don't have to hurt you. Just let me have the kid. You know I can't let her go." His voice was very low and calm. Natalie stared in disbelief as she shook her head. There was no way she would let him touch Shelly. She would die first. Tears began to stream down her cheeks with the realization that she was powerless against him. She had seen him fighting with Rick, heard the way Rick had described his strength and abilities. Her chest felt empty, her head a little dizzy. The air suddenly seemed very thin. Each breath too shallow. *Lord, please help us. Don't let him get to her. Show me how to stop him.*

When she didn't respond or move aside, his dark eyes tensed and his voice became forceful. "What did she tell the police?" He moved closer. "How detailed was her description? Do they know who she saw?" He was getting louder now.

Natalie shook her head, trying to hold it together. "She didn't see you clearly. She didn't tell them anything useful." Her voice was practically pleading. It wasn't a lie. Shelly's description could have fit at least a third of the men in Maple Rapids. Never mind the surrounding towns. Nothing she said had been all that pertinent. The real threat Shelly posed was that she could identify him if she saw him again.

"You're lying!" He edged closer. "Tell me what she said!" He was yelling now. He seemed so angry. His deep booming voice felt as though it was prickling against her skin. She wanted to take Shelly and run, but that was impossible within the confines of her cottage. He had her cornered.

Natalie shifted out of the doorway, trying to draw him into the living room, away from Shelly. "I saw more than she did. I saw you in the river with that woman. I watched her fight for her life. I was right there. I know what you look like!" Shelly was the one to have witnessed the struggle, but if Natalie could draw him away by pretending she had been there, too, maybe she could buy some time until help arrived. Pete had promised he'd check on them. She prayed it was soon. "I'm the one you should worry about!" Then she ran, hoping he would follow. He didn't hesitate. Heavy footsteps pounded the wood floors behind her. Ignoring the pain in her foot, she scurried into the kitchen and her eyes quickly searched the wood block on the counter for the one large knife that had been there since she moved in six months ago. It was missing. Her mind reeled before she remembered it was inside the dishwasher. No time to pull it open and slide out a rack. She randomly grabbed a handle and then shuffled to the other side of the table.

"The police are right outside. All I have to do is scream." That thought finally occurred to her. Maybe it would be enough to get him to leave if she let out a screech loud enough to bring the officers inside. She widened her stance and held up the knife, bracing for whatever he might do.

A deep chuckle rumbled from his throat. Then he spoke in a low tone that was half whisper and half growl. "Scream all you want. No one's coming." Then he laughed some more while he shifted his body back and forth as if he was about to come around the table, like it was a game. Her legs tensed. She swayed from side to side, mirroring his movements, as she tried to anticipate what he would do. He didn't seem to have an ounce of hesitation. If anything, he was emboldened by what he was planning to do, even more so than he had been the night before. "You should have just let me have the kid. This whole thing would have been over. Now, you've left me no choice. I won't stop 'til you're both dead." There was so much certainty in his voice. It was so cold and absolute.

Natalie felt a chill shimmy down her spine. Why was he so sure that the police wouldn't come if she screamed? Then, far worse thoughts took over. Who would take care of Shelly if she died? What were the chances her niece would see tomorrow if that happened? She had to find a way to distract him. To draw this out long enough for help to arrive. But how? She had no idea when Officer Dennis would show up. He could be busy for hours before he thought to check in. He would probably want to get some sleep after the night he had.

The masked man's eyes were dark, like Shelly had described to Officer Dennis. A deep brown that made it difficult to see his pupils. There seemed to be determination in the slant of his eyebrows. Whatever the reasons for what he had done and was trying to do now, she got the sense that there was a specific motivation that drove his actions. None of that changed the reality of his intentions. Natalie began to regret listening to Officer Dennis when he said he didn't feel it would be unsafe to come back to the cottage. There had been no signs of a break-in when the officers had checked, but that was clearly no indication of what the masked man knew. The officers out front were supposed to be nothing more than a precaution. Maybe that had been what drew the killer's attention to where Natalie and Shelly were. Or maybe he had access to information that made it impossible for them to be safe anywhere in Maple Rapids.

Looking down at the two-inch blade of the knife she had grabbed, she inwardly groaned. It was the smallest in the set. The least effective in her current situation. She slid it into her sweatpants pocket, knowing it would be useless against him, then picked up the chair in front of her and flung it over the table. He lifted his hand and deflected it away as if it weighed nothing. The chair crashed to the floor. Natalie grabbed the wooden handle that had looked the same as those attached to much larger blades, and held it up again, praying there was a way to survive this.

Knowing that the so-called weapon in her hand wasn't going to do anything except maybe buy her a moment or two if she managed to cut him deep enough to distract him. Then she heard Shelly call out from the bedroom. The man swiveled his head in that direction and then back to her. The resolve in his eyes seemed to intensify. His head tilted slightly to one side as he stared at Natalie. As though her fear was somehow entertaining.

Shelly had already come too close to death six months ago. Natalie hadn't fought her way through the hot flames and smoke, smashed through the living-room window and gotten her niece out moments before the interior of the house collapsed to watch her die now. The memory of it made her knees feel weak. When Shelly peeked around the corner from the hallway, it was impossible to keep the panic from her expression. The masked man turned, following the line of her gaze. She took advantage of his momentary distraction and shoved the table at him with as much force as she could muster. It hit him hard and knocked him slightly to one side. When he turned back, he glared at her, his eyes filled with rage. Then he grabbed the edge of the table and flipped it over. It smacked into the wall and dropped with a clatter before it settled on an angle. He stared for a moment and then walked directly toward her. She held up the useless little knife and braced for the worst. Before he could touch her, she screamed out, "Shelly! Run! Hide!" She was hoping that Shelly would go outside to the police car and find safety. She had to be okay.

Familiar panic seeped into her muscles. It was similar to the night her brother and his wife died. That sense of helplessness. The absolute desperation to keep Shelly from harm. What were the chances she could do it again?

The fire had very nearly taken them both down. This was worse. A dangerous man who was determined to kill them wouldn't stop coming. There was no slipping outside for safety. He would follow. A lump formed in her throat. He was moving closer, pushing a similar heat against her skin.

The masked man grabbed her wrist with such force that the knife fell from her grasp. She could see her niece staring with terror etched all over her face as the killer wrapped his hand around Natalie's neck. She kicked wildly and clawed at his gloved hand but nothing worked. He was unmovable. Natalie waved her hand toward Shelly, praying that she would understand that she had to run. But she didn't. Instead, that brave little girl marched right over to them and kicked the masked man in the back of his leg.

She screamed, "Let Aunt Natty go!" Shelly's face had morphed into an anger Natalie had never seen in her before. The fear was still there, but she was too young to realize how precarious her situation was.

He released his grip on Natalie's throat as he turned to grab Shelly. Terrified what might happen, ignoring the way her oxygen-deprived body screamed for air, Natalie reared back her leg and slammed her knee between his legs with everything she had. Then she bellowed with what was left of her voice.

"Shelly, you have to run and hide! Now!" The hoarseness felt like razors in her throat.

Shelly's little eyes widened and then she was off. The masked man watched Shelly dash into the hallway and then focused all of his wrath back on Natalie. She had clearly missed her target. He didn't seem the least bit deterred and there was fire in his eyes now. His hand snapped back up to Natalie's neck and he thrust her into the wall. The room was shrinking into darkness, her lungs

Addie Ellis

fighting for air. She was nearly unconscious when she felt her body crash to the floor. All she could think about was Shelly. No one was there to protect her. Natalie wanted to get up and fight. To scream for the police to come inside. Why hadn't they heard her when she yelled for Shelly to run? Why hadn't they come running? Thoughts swirled into the murkiness enveloping her. She was slipping into oblivion. Darkness closed in on the room, and then she was gone.

The road curved into the wooded part of town as Rick drove higher up the mountain. There were several fallen tree limbs from the storm that had lashed through the area the night before. It had gotten significantly worse while they were in the police station. It wasn't a surprise to see so much debris along the sides of the road. He had heard Natalie tell Pete where she lived. Growing up, he had spent several weeks every summer in the cabin and knew exactly where her little cottage was. She had covered a lot of rough terrain to get to his place last night. Not an easy thing to do with a young child. Maybe Pete was right to assume the killer didn't know where they lived. Given how far they ran to get to his cabin, the masked man wouldn't have any reason to think they lived out that way. Even if he thought to check, there were a lot of other cottages in the little neighborhood that lined the river on that edge of town.

He pulled to a stop on the street out front and turned off the truck. There were two police officers sitting in the black-and-white car in the driveway next to a small crossover SUV that was farther back. The police car was backed in and angled away from where Rick had parked. He could see the driver's side and the two men sitting inside. Natalie's cottage was about fifty yards from the river that cut through the woods and wrapped around other parts of the town. It was a small white structure with flower boxes below the windows. He had been in several such cottages as a child when he made friends with other kids staying in town with their families.

He stared through the passenger-side window of his truck, looking around the outside of the house, trying to make sense of the sick feeling dropping into his stomach and tensing his body. Everything looked fine. The curtains were drawn. Nothing was out of place. Rick glanced back at the police car. Something was off there. The two men inside hadn't moved. They were too still. They hadn't even turned in his direction when he pulled up. Then his gaze shifted to the other vehicle in the driveway. It was pulled closer to the cottage. The two tires he could see were both flat. Rick's hand reached for the door handle without thought. Everything inside him began to shift. He jumped from the truck and ran toward the police car with a sense of foreboding he hadn't felt in four years. Not since that night overseas when he lost most of his unit. Everything inside him was dreading what he would find. But there was no turning back now.

Rick peered into the window of the police car and what he saw made his blood run cold. It was happening again. He was too late. They were both dead. Each with a bullet hole in the center of the forehead. He turned and saw the corresponding holes in the windshield. This was an experienced shooter. Someone who could make a shot from a distance. The shooter had to have taken cover in the trees across the street to do it without being noticed. Otherwise the officers would have seen him coming and taken action. This wouldn't narrow things down. There were several seasoned hunters in town with this level of skill. The officer in the passenger seat had clearly been reaching for his gun but hadn't been fast enough. It was unlikely he would have known where the shot came from with any real accuracy. He would have had a better chance of survival if he had dropped down low.

Rick grabbed the radio in the car and pressed the button. "This is Rick Barrett. I'm at Natalie's cottage. Both officers are dead. I'm going inside." Then he dropped the radio and ran up the front walk without waiting for a response. When he reached the front door, he kicked it in. The moment he stepped inside, he came face-to-face with the masked man.

A quick scan of the room was enough to send him into full fight mode. Natalie was on the floor. Her neck looked bruised from where he stood. He was too late to save her. Where was Shelly? He turned back to the masked man, ready to take him on. The pain of failing again was insurmountable. The killer took a step back.

"This has nothing to do with you. Just leave." There was that strange voice again. There was nothing familiar about it. Not like those dark eyes. Something in them was gnawing at Rick.

"Where's Shelly?" He feared the answer. When the man said nothing, Rick took a step closer, intent on getting a response. The masked man was unmoving, his stocky build even bigger than Rick had realized in the dark the night before. A sudden quick punch hit Rick in the gut. He went to hit back, but the man stepped out of the way and grabbed Rick from the side, trapping his arms against his body.

"Just stop. Don't fight it. Leave. Don't make me hurt you, too." In answer, Rick attempted to slam his head sideways into the killer's masked face, but he turned and Rick's head hit near the man's ear. He quickly stomped his heel down on the man's foot, causing his grip to loosen, and Rick shifted out of his grasp. He grabbed the man by his black shirt and smashed him into the wall. How could he actually believe Rick would walk away and do nothing to stop a killer?

"Where is Shelly?" Rick ground out the words, his anger over Natalie fueling his strength and determination. He had thrown the man into the Sheetrock as if he was half his actual size. Rick had known loss and frustration but it had never hit him like this. Natalie and Shelly were innocent. They hadn't chosen to put themselves in danger. They were gentle and good. With Natalie lying on the floor, possibly dead, it was difficult not to do something much worse. He felt something in his spirit pulling on him. Stopping him just short of ending this in seconds with a quick maneuver.

A groan from across the room pulled Rick's attention away from the criminal in his grasp. Natalie was alive. Relief flooded his veins. Her head moved just a little. Another raspy groan slipped from her soft lips. Then the sound of police sirens echoed through the house from up the road. Rick turned back to the masked man.

"Where's the little girl? What have you done with her?" He got no answer. Just a cold stare from those deep brown eyes. There was a darkness there that had nothing to do with the color. Movement from where Natalie was had Rick turning to see if she was alright. The assailant took advantage of this temporary distraction and shoved Rick aside, then ran out the door. Rick wanted to follow. To pull that mask from the other man's head and stop him.

He couldn't risk leaving Natalie. Her injuries could be serious.

He rushed across the room and kneeled by her side. His fingers reached out gently to brush the dark curls out of her face. "Are you okay? Natalie, please open your eyes." He waited, looking down at the bruising that spanned the width of her neck. The next time he came face-to-face with that man, he wouldn't ask questions. He was going to take him down no matter what it took. *Please, help her. Please, let Shelly be safe.*

The sound of cars pulling up and then the voices of the police officers could be heard from outside. Natalie opened her eyes. She tried to speak but her voice was strained.

"Where's Shelly?" Tears streamed down her temples.

Rick shook his head. "I don't know. I haven't seen her. She wasn't with the masked man when he ran out of here. I'll find her."

Pete Dennis ran inside with four other officers behind him. One had been in the store talking to Dan Caraway this morning. Pete walked over to Rick and Natalie the moment he saw them. "How is she?"

Rick wasn't sure how to answer since he didn't know. He shook his head with all of the anguish still rushing through his veins at the sight of Natalie on the floor when he walked in. Never mind the building fear for Shelly's safety. "I'm not sure. She just woke up. Her voice is weak. I think he tried to strangle her. She needs an ambulance." When Pete nodded, Rick added, "He ran out of here a few seconds before you pulled up. He could still be close."

Pete turned to the other officers. He pointed at two of them and said, "You two, go outside and look. Find him." He kneeled down beside Rick. "Miss Owens? Can you hear me?"

Natalie blinked up at him. She mouthed the word *Shelly*. Pete got on his radio and called for paramedics. Then he asked Rick, "Where's the little girl?"

"I haven't seen her. I haven't looked around yet."

Pete told the remaining two officers to split off and search inside and outside the house. When Natalie tried to sit up, Pete gently pressed down on her shoulders. "I don't think you should move until we get you checked out."

She pushed her way up. "It was only my neck." She rubbed her fingers tenderly over the bruising around her throat. "I have to find Shelly." Her voice was a little better than a rough whisper now.

"You stay here. I'll look for her." Rick stood up, wanting to do something useful. He hoped his delayed arrival hadn't been too late. He shouldn't have taken the long way. He shouldn't have hesitated. It was selfish. He had allowed his own issues to get in the way of doing what he knew was right.

When Natalie nodded, he started moving through the hallway. He checked the room that looked to be Shelly's first. There was a stuffed bear on the unmade bed and her dirty slippers from last night were on the floor. There was nothing under the bed. The closet had already been cleared by Officer Hazel Clarke. She stood watching Rick look where she had already been. He ran across the hall into what he presumed to be Natalie's room. There was nothing under the bed or in the closet. He let out an exasperated sigh. Then he noticed a pile of blankets in the corner. He quickly started pulling them apart but there was no adorable little girl hiding beneath.

Back out in the hallway, Rick scanned the space, hoping there was something that Hazel missed. Some small corner where Shelly had been able to hide. He looked in the bathroom and then pulled open the hall closet. He started to shift a large package of toilet paper on the floor, but stopped when he heard whimpering. Then he pulled the package out of the way. The floor behind it was empty.

"Shelly, are you in here? It's Rick. You're safe. The masked man is gone." Just then, Natalie hobbled into the hallway.

"Shelly?" Her voice was still raspy, but improving. Clearly, Pete hadn't been able to stop Natalie from looking for her niece.

A moment later, a large blanket fell from the first shelf and hit the floor. Shelly squirmed out and ran into Natalie's arms as she dropped to her knees. "I hid, like you said."

"You did a great job." Natalie pulled her niece closer, tears spilling down her cheeks. "I'm so proud of you."

Pete came into the hallway. "The paramedics are here. Please, let them look at you."

Rick moved to Natalie's side and helped her stand back up. He put his arm around her waist and guided her out to the ambulance, with Shelly at her other side, their hands clasped together. While the paramedics looked Natalie and Shelly over, again, Rick told Pete how he found the officers out front and about his interaction with the masked man.

"Did you recognize him?" Pete looked hopeful.

Rick shook his head. "There was something about his eyes but I can't be sure if I've actually met him. They're dark brown, which is pretty common. What I will say is that he didn't want to engage with me. He told me to stay out of it. That he didn't want to hurt me. He disguised his voice again. I can't shake this strange feeling. I just don't know what it is."

When Natalie stepped off the back of the ambulance, with the help of one of the paramedics, she and Shelly walked toward Rick and Pete. Even ambling with a limp, there was a sense of urgency to her movements. She was focused on Pete. Rick couldn't help but wonder what she was about to say. Then one of the officers Pete sent out to look for the masked man came running from the woods. He was yelling something that had everyone turning to look. Had he found the killer? Had he been able to do what Rick hadn't?

SIX

Natalie turned when she heard yelling and reached to pull Shelly close to her. A police officer came running from the trees across the street, his hand clutched around something dark. She noticed Officer Pete Dennis moving his hand toward the gun on his hip, his index finger twitching near the grip. Rick stepped in front of Natalie and Shelly, his stance wide. He seemed to be intent on shielding them from whatever might be about to happen.

The officer stopped running as he reached the street. He held up his hand, letting a black ski mask hang in front of him. "I nearly had him. He knocked me down and was gone before I could get a look at his face." His cheeks were red with effort and his stocky frame moved with strength.

Officer Dennis relaxed his hand. "What happened?"

"I was nearly on him when he realized I was comin' and he just took off. I caught up and we went at it for a minute. I got hold of the mask from the back. He must have felt it. He whipped me into a tree and took off. I managed to keep hold of the mask. Maybe we can pull hair or saliva." He shook his head, dejected. "I didn't see his face. Just some short dark hair, like the kid said. He's a tough one, I'll tell you. I haven't gone up against one like him before."

Officer Dennis turned toward Natalie and Shelly. "Either of you get a look this time?"

Natalie shook her head. "He had the mask on." She hadn't thought to pull it off when he had her pinned by her neck against the wall. Now, she wished she had.

Rick turned to the officer holding the mask. "Dave, did he say anything to you?"

Dave was shaking his head. "Not a word."

Officer Dennis spoke up. "Get that mask bagged. Put a rush on it with the lab."

The officer nodded and jogged over to his police cruiser.

Natalie lifted Shelly into her arms. "I'm going inside to pack. I'm getting my niece far away from here. I'll call if Shelly remembers anything else." She started walking toward the cottage that had been like a small haven for the last six months. Now, it was nothing more than another bad memory. Probably something that would haunt her dreams, like the fire.

Officer Dennis's voice halted her in place. "I'm sorry, but that isn't going to be possible."

Natalie turned, ready to argue until she saw the remorse in his eyes. "This isn't about Shelly being your only witness, is it?"

"I wish it were. I'd drive you out of here myself until this guy is caught. That storm damaged the only bridge in and out of town. I'd have you taken out by boat but the river is too rough. It wouldn't be safe. For now, we need to protect you somewhere here in Maple Rapids."

Natalie could feel the anxiety pulling and weighing on every part of her body. She put Shelly down. The pain and exhaustion was making her weak. How much more of this could they endure? Especially Shelly. She felt a knot forming in her throat. It was beginning to feel hopeless. She took in a steadying breath. "So what now?"

"Pack a bag and we'll take you to a motel on the outskirts of town. I'll have an officer on the door at all times. Only one way in and out. One of us will be on it." Pete Dennis turned toward Hazel Clarke. "The guys in the cruiser were shot from over there, based on the angle of entry through the windshield." He pointed toward an area of trees across the street. "Go see if our guy left any casings."

Officer Clarke pulled rubber gloves from her pocket, put them on and walked across the street. She moved slowly, her head bent low, as she carefully examined every inch of the ground.

Rick moved to Natalie's side. His soft green eyes were filled with intensity. "I'd like to be there. Let me help protect you."

Natalie's instinct was to say no. She wasn't used to depending on anyone but her big brother. She didn't have him anymore and she'd been struggling with feeling lost since he died. Now, there was this brave man willing to keep putting himself in harm's way to save her and Shelly. How could she keep letting him do it? He wasn't her family. Despite that, she needed him. Shelly needed him. She sent up a quick prayer as she nodded her consent. *Please, don't let any harm come to this man. His relentless willingness to step in front of danger over and over for us makes him worthy of Your protection. Please, don't let him get hurt.*

The look of relief on Rick's face was baffling to her, but all she could feel was gratitude filling her insides. She started walking inside, Shelly's hand in hers, to pack a bag, when she remembered what she had been intent on saying before the officer came running out of the woods. She turned back to Officer Dennis and Rick. "I think he's local."

Officer Dennis stepped closer. "Why do you say that?"

"When he was yelling at me, he asked about Shelly's description of him. Then he asked if they know who she saw, I guess meaning the police. Like the description would be enough for you to identify him."

Officer Dennis scrubbed his hands down his face as he let out an exasperated breath. "So he's someone we know. That's very... This definitely changes the way we'll be looking at things now." He rubbed the back of his head as he seemed to ponder this new development.

Hazel walked over to Officer Dennis holding a little baggie. "I've got two casings. And, yes, I took pictures before I picked them up. I think he makes his own bullets. One is cracked." Natalie wondered how that helped her come to that conclusion. She didn't know anything about guns or bullets. She never needed to before.

Officer Dennis took a look. "You're probably right. Get them to the lab. If it doesn't match anything in the system, see if we can get some casings from the range to compare them to." She nodded and headed to her car.

Natalie heard Rick talking to Officer Dennis as she walked inside with Shelly to pack. He said, "Is there anyone jumping to mind? Maybe someone with a criminal past?"

"Not that I can think of. I've known these people for years, which makes the idea a little tough to wrap my head around. And let's be honest. There're a lot of guys that fit. And they all know their way around guns." Officer Dennis's words were a little strained. She didn't hear any more of the conversation once she was inside.

Cops were still processing the scene, using words she'd never heard anywhere but on television before all of this. She'd been part of a crime scene twice in less than twenty-four hours. How was that even possible?

It didn't take long to gather their personal belongings. They hadn't brought much when they came last spring. Natalie never thought they'd be here this long. A medium duffel bag each and they were out the door with no intention of ever returning to this cottage. Once she was back outside, she started heading to her car. That's when she realized all of her tires had been slashed. This guy really knew how to cover all of his bases.

"You can ride with me." Rick came over and took the duffel bags off Natalie's shoulder. "We'll deal with your tires later. They'll get to work on the bridge right away. I'm sure it'll be passable within a week or so."

"If we're still alive that long." She hadn't meant to say that out loud. She knew Rick meant well.

"I won't let anything happen to either of you. I'm with you to the end." He sounded so absolute. Something shifted in his eyes. A coldness. Maybe that wasn't right. It was a level of seriousness Natalie wasn't used to. Then again, she had never been in a situation like this before. She could really see the soldier in him now. She could almost see that part of him that did things to save others. Things that soldiers sometimes had to do to survive. It wasn't a darkness but it had a similar weight. She felt as though it should scare her, but all it did was make her feel like she and Shelly might actually survive this.

As they drove away in Rick's truck, with Officer Dennis driving ahead of them and another cruiser driven by the officer they called Hazel at their rear, she looked back at the cottage. At the flurry of activity moving in and out through the front door. There was something about it that didn't sit right. Her stomach was twisting but she couldn't figure out why. Then she saw the smoke.

When Pete's cruiser stopped short in front of them, Rick's truck nearly ran into it. Pete got out and came running to Rick's door. He rolled down the window.

"He set the place on fire. I just got the call. I need to make sure everyone is okay and see if we can track this guy. He's getting pretty bold. I don't know how he did it without being seen. There must be evidence inside that he doesn't want us to find. Hazel is going to take you to the motel and get you settled. Dave Salomon will meet you there. He's the one that got the mask off the assailant. He'll be taking the first watch. I sent him earlier to set up a room and make sure it was secure. I'll come by later." He tapped his hand twice on the doorframe and then ran back to his car, quickly turned it around and drove back toward Natalie's cottage.

Rick turned to check on Natalie and saw her hand covering her mouth. Her other arm was wrapped tightly around Shelly, who had taken the center of the bench seat in his truck. He wasn't sure how to comfort her. He had to focus on getting them far from the danger. He couldn't let any emotion come into this. It would make him less effective. He had to stay alert. Aware of everything around them. Worrying about Natalie's or Shelly's feelings would only serve as a distraction. He couldn't fail them.

Hazel pulled around the truck and led the way to the motel. She took them through some winding roads, higher and deeper into the woods. When they pulled into the motel parking lot, Dave Salomon was there waiting. His cruiser was tucked between two other cars under an overhanging tree. He stood from a chair positioned outside one of the doors.

Rick parked on the other side of one of the cars near the cruiser, trying to put it out of view from the street. The motel was a red U-shaped structure sided with painted wood that had worn over the years. A shallow porch lined the front with a small sets of steps from the gravel in front of each door. It was tucked into the trees with the front being the only part not facing forest. There were other cars parked in front of some of the doors, which meant they weren't the only guests staying here. He wasn't sure if it was a good idea to risk being this close to other people but he supposed there weren't very many options in a small town like Maple Rapids.

"Is this really a good idea? Shouldn't we be looking for a place where other people won't get caught in the middle if he finds us here?" Natalie was looking around, her eyebrows pinched together.

"I was thinking the same thing but maybe it's a positive. More potential witnesses might keep him from making a move on this place." He knew that it wasn't likely going to act as a deterrent given how brazen this guy had already been. The fact that his response seemed to give Natalie a little comfort was at least something.

Hazel walked them toward the room, where Dave was standing. He opened the door as they approached and handed Rick a key.

"I've cleared it. Not that the guy would know to look here yet."

Rick caught the word *yet*. He didn't like their odds.

Natalie brought Shelly inside and turned to Dave. "How long will we be here?"

"Until we can get you out of town. If the river settles

down, we'll take you out by boat. Otherwise, we have to wait for the bridge. We'll coordinate with your local police to set up protective custody in your hometown once we can get you out."

As she nodded and went farther into the room, Rick looked around at their surroundings. There were a lot of trees. Which meant a lot of places for the masked man to hide and wait to make a move. "Do you have anyone at the rear?"

"It's a little high in the back. He won't be coming in that way. The windows are small and up too high. If he makes a move, it'll be from the front." Dave sat down in the chair. "I'll be right here with my weapon at the ready." He held his pistol in his lap, his finger running along the barrel. "Someone will bring some food in a couple hours if you're hungry. Let Pete know what everyone wants."

Rick nodded, went in and closed the door. He put the bags and the box of cereal he picked up earlier on a small table with three chairs. He brought his go bag in with their duffels. There were two double beds covered with old floral bedspreads. The tan carpet was worn but clean, like everything else in the room. He walked over and looked out the back window. Dave was right. It was a bit of a drop back there. Unless the guy brought a ladder, he'd have to come through the front.

"Why don't you get some rest?" Natalie was looking at him. "I know you haven't slept yet. Shelly and I can take this bed and you can take the other." She nodded toward the one closer to the front of the room.

"That might be a good idea. If he does find us, it probably won't be for a little while. Meanwhile, Dave is ready for whatever comes out there. All of the cops will want to get this guy now that he's killed two of them." He didn't bother to pull down the bedspread or take off his shoes. He lay on top, his pistol at his side. He kept his hand over it, ready to move. "By the way, I picked up the cereal Shelly was asking for. It's on the table if she's hungry." He closed his eyes. He knew how to fall asleep fast. His time in the service had taught him to take sleep when he could get it. "You should try to sleep, too. Don't unpack. Be ready to move at a moment's notice." Then he let himself drift off without looking to see if he'd caused any alarm.

He had no doubt that the masked man would be coming. That he would find them. This guy was smart and capable. Rick couldn't help but wonder if the killer might have a military or law-enforcement background. He figured Pete Dennis would have the same thoughts and start running background checks on all of the men in town that met the description and had the abilities. Now, Rick needed to rest so he would be ready when the killer made his next move.

SEVEN

A sudden pounding on the door startled Natalie out of her slumber. She sat up in bed, trying to get her bearings. The space was unfamiliar. It took a few seconds to remember that she was in the motel. Shelly was still asleep. Rick was already on his feet, peering out through a slim opening in the curtain.

"It's Pete." Rick opened the door and stepped aside as Pete came in carrying bags of food from a local restaurant. The smell filled the room, making Natalie's belly grumble. She couldn't remember the last time she ate.

Rick moved the duffel bags off the table so Pete could set down the food. "Any news? Did you find him?"

"I wish I had good news. There were no matches on the casings. We're going to check some other avenues to find something on that. We're hoping the ski mask will have something and that our guy is in the system. If he's not, it won't matter what we find." He turned to Natalie. "Are you hungry? I brought plenty."

She got off the bed and pulled the food out of the bags. Shelly sat up and came over to see what Officer Denis brought. When Natalie found a container with chicken fingers and fries, she set it in front of Shelly, who was now sitting in one of the chairs.

Officer Dennis and Rick were off in one corner of the room talking in hushed tones. Natalie wasn't sure if she wanted to know what they were saying. It wouldn't change anything. When Pete left, he told them he'd be back in the morning. That was when Natalie realized it was almost dark outside. That Rick must have turned on the lights at some point before she woke up. They had slept through what was left of the day.

"Would you like something to eat? There's a burger, a chicken dish, some other things I haven't opened yet." Natalie turned to Rick.

"I'll take whatever you ladies don't want." He sat on the edge of the bed. "Pete has some leads. Maybe we'll be out of here by morning."

"What kind of leads?" Natalie brought the container with the burger and fries over to Rick. "Are you a burger guy?"

He nodded and took the food. "Thanks. He's running checks on everyone who fits the profile in town. He should have the warrant for the shooting range soon. Matching casings there will be like finding a needle in a haystack but at least it could narrow his search. He's pushing hard on this. Looking at every possible angle. He seems to think he'll get the go-ahead before the night is out."

"I hope he finds this guy fast. I don't think it'll be hard for him to find us here. There aren't very many places to look in a town like this. Especially since there is an officer posted outside the door." Natalie sat at the table and started eating. "Anything else?"

"He's got a few other things going. Not sure they'll lead anywhere. And don't worry. This place is pretty tucked away. The officer is in plain clothes and the car is hidden from the street. Hopefully, this will be over tonight, anyway."

Natalie nodded. There wasn't much to say about it. All she could do was wait and see what came next. For now, she would focus on making this less stressful for Shelly. And getting cleaned up. "Would you mind if I took a shower after we eat?"

"Of course not. Why would I mind?" Rick didn't seem to understand why she was asking.

"Let me rephrase. Would you mind keeping Shelly company while I take a shower?" She smiled when Shelly lit up and looked over toward Rick.

"I think I can do that. I'm sure we can find something to occupy ourselves for a little while." He brought his food over to the table just as Natalie stood up. They nearly ran into each other. Stopping just inches apart, Natalie looked up into Rick's green eyes. They still held no fear. All she could see was kindness. It was almost hard to look away. There seemed to be something else there. Something she couldn't identify.

"I won't be long." Natalie moved aside so Rick could sit down.

"Take your time. We'll be right here."

"Can we play a game?" Shelly gave him a shy smile as she asked. She seemed to like Rick and that made Natalie happy. It also made her miss her brother a little more. He would never be able to play a game with his daughter, or see her grow up. It was a reminder that Natalie didn't have any family left. She didn't know Rick well enough to really count him as a friend. She trusted that he'd fight for them when the situation warranted, but beyond that, he had a life of his own.

Just as Natalie was about to step into the bathroom,

something hit the outside door, hard. She turned and saw Rick was already on his feet. Shelly ran to Natalie. She lifted her niece into her arms as Rick edged toward the window to look outside. When he reached for the corner of the curtain, something scraped against the outside of the door. Rick turned to Natalie and waved his hand, signaling for her to take Shelly into the bathroom. She moved quickly and closed the door as quietly as possible. She was surrounded by white tile. It covered the floor and walls. The tub was white with a clear shower curtain. No windows. Nowhere to go if this went wrong. She pressed herself against the far wall and said a prayer for Rick and for the policeman posted outside. What felt like an eternity later, she noticed the door handle turning. The only question was, who was on the other side?

Shelly's scream startled Rick as he pushed open the door. He held up his hands to calm down the child and a white-faced, breathless Natalie.

"It's okay. The officer outside tripped and fell into the door. His chair got knocked over and he dragged it back into place. The back scraped against the door when he was picking it up. I didn't mean to scare you. I was just trying to keep things quiet in here. I don't want anyone to know we're here. If they mention it to the wrong person in town, that could bring the killer to us."

"I get it, but you might have at least said something outside the door before opening it. I had no way of knowing it was you." Natalie's tone was less angry than scared. He couldn't blame her. She probably felt cornered.

Rick nodded. "I will announce myself if we find ourselves in this position again." He looked down at Shelly as she stepped from behind Natalie. "Are you ready to play some cards?" When she nodded and reached out her little hand, he took it in his. The way Shelly curled her fingers around two of his sent a flurry of emotion through him. He was beginning to care about them. He couldn't allow that. He couldn't become attached. They were targets of a killer. A killer that was determined to take them out. His heart pounded against the thought. The only option was to stay detached.

Turning back to Natalie, Rick said, "We'll be out here. Take your time." Her expression was filled with angst. Was she able to tell what he was thinking? Was she still rattled by the way he opened the door? Then he noticed sadness in her eyes. "Are you okay?" When she nodded and smiled, he walked Shelly back over to the table. She seemed to have recovered quickly.

"What will we play? Go Fish?" She said it with excitement. He couldn't help but admire the kid's resilience.

"Whatever you like. I think I saw a deck of cards…" He reached into the top drawer of the dresser. "Yup, here they are." He had thoroughly examined the entire room when he woke from his nap earlier.

Shelly was eager to play. She wanted to deal the cards and was very creative with the rules she kept creating for the purpose of getting an advantage. The chatter was light and she even giggled a few times. Then she looked up at Rick with her eyebrows pressed together.

"Are your mom and dad still alive?" There was so much to that question. He knew more would come once he answered and didn't feel that it was his place to have a conversation like this with her.

He glanced over to the bathroom door. He could still hear the water running. There was no way to pass this over to Natalie. He turned back to Shelly. Those big brown eyes blinked up at him.

"Mine died. Now, Aunt Natty doesn't want to go home."

Rick took one more look toward the bathroom. There was no avoiding this conversation. Or the potential minefield of emotion it could unlock in both of them. Never mind how Natalie might feel about it.

EIGHT

Once Natalie was clean and dressed in fresh clothes, it felt as though the day had been washed away. As if things could finally start getting better. She had spent some time in prayer while showering and felt a little rejuvenated. As she combed her wet hair, she heard Rick and Shelly's voices. She cracked open the door to hear what they were talking about.

"It's really hard to lose someone you care about," Rick said. "Even though the people I lost weren't family, I do have an idea of what you're feeling. The thing that you should try to remember is that even though they're gone, you will always have them with you in your heart. And you can take comfort in knowing they are with God. There is no better place. Try to remember that they're a part of who you are. Even I can see what kind of people they were by looking at you." Rick sounded more gentle than Natalie would have thought possible.

"But you never met them," Shelly said. Natalie's heart dropped into the pit of her stomach. Shelly hadn't mentioned her parents to Natalie in a couple of months. Why were they talking about this now? Had Rick said something to upset her?

"No, but I know they were good people because of

what a sweet girl you are. And smart, too." He actually seemed to know exactly what to say.

Next came one of Shelly's giggles. One Natalie hadn't heard since the fire. She eased the door open. Then Rick said something that didn't make much sense, but it had Shelly in a full belly laugh. He was so good with her. It filled Natalie with a strange emotion. Something foreign but warm. When she heard the roar of Rick's chuckle, she couldn't resist stepping out to see what they were doing.

Walking into the room, she said, "What's going on out here?" It was impossible to contain the smile that broke out across her face.

Rick turned toward her with a kind of lightness in his expression. The heaviness of the day seemed to have been lifted for him, too. "Well, your niece is rather creative with her rules. A game of Go Fish has devolved into something quite different. I dare to say that she might have a new game that other kids would want to play."

"Really? How fun. Will you teach me?" Natalie walked toward the table.

"Sit with me, Aunt Natty. I'll show you. We can beat Rick together." Then she giggled some more. Natalie hadn't seen Shelly laugh or joke around this way since that last night before losing her parents. They had all played *Monopoly* at the kitchen table before going to bed. It was a reminder of better times. It was also a comfort to realize that Shelly's last memory of them was a happy one.

Watching the banter between Rick and Shelly triggered a memory of her niece trying to get Natalie's ex, Eric, to play cards with her. He was never willing to play any games. He had barely wanted to deal with talking to Shelly. Seeing the way Rick embraced all of the silliness made Natalie realize, for the first time, that Eric wouldn't have been good with kids. So he wouldn't have been the kind of father she would have hoped for if they'd had children of their own. How had she missed that?

They continued to play pretty late into the night. Since they had all slept through the afternoon, it wasn't until after midnight that Shelly began to show signs of winding down. When she yawned and rubbed her eyes, Natalie knew it was time to wrap things up. Not that she wanted to.

"I think it might be time to get some sleep." She rubbed Shelly's back.

Shelly groaned, "Do I have to?"

"We can play again tomorrow, assuming Rick doesn't mind?" She turned toward him.

"Are you kidding? Bring it on. We can experiment with all of the rules you want to make." He grinned at Shelly.

"Really? You'll play again?"

"Of course. Now, I think you better rest that big brain so you can teach us something new tomorrow." Rick stood up.

Shelly hurried over to the bed she'd slept in earlier and scurried under the blankets. "I'm going to make a whole new game tomorrow."

Natalie tucked her in and kissed her forehead. "That sounds like a great idea."

Shelly's arms wrapped around Natalie's neck. "Good night. I love you, Aunt Natty."

"I love you, too." How was it that such a horrible experience had somehow made things between them better than it had been in months?

"Good night, Rick."

"Good night, Peanut." Rick walked over and stood next to Natalie. "Dream of something wonderful." This had

Natalie's eyes nearly tearing up. Did he know that Shelly's father had called her *Peanut*? Did she tell him? Or was it merely a coincidence?

They both took their seats at the table while Shelly fell asleep. Natalie cleaned up the cards and put them back into the drawer Rick indicated when she was looking to put them away. It was so quiet without Shelly's laughter filling the emptiness of the motel room. It brought the reality of why they were there back into focus. Natalie wanted this to be over. Not because she didn't enjoy Rick's company. She did, but it was the situation that had brought them together that she wanted to be done with. Watching him with Shelly that evening had been the perfect distraction. She was about to ask if he was tired when he cleared his throat.

"When you were in the shower Shelly started talking to me about her parents and wanting to go home. I hope I didn't overstep but I spoke to her about some of it. I didn't want to make her feel worse by avoiding it. I hope that's okay." His eyes held uncertainty.

Natalie laced her fingers together in front of her, as though she was about to pray, and rubbed her palms back and forth against each other. It was something she sometimes did when she was stressed or thinking about something that required focus. "I only heard the last thing you said. It sounded like you gave her exactly what she needed. How much did she tell you?"

He blew out a breath. "I'm glad you aren't angry. I wasn't sure it was my place but that kid is hard to resist. She asked if my parents were alive. She talked about things she used to do with her parents. It sounds like you've always been a big part of her life. She mentioned you in just about every memory. She talked about wanting to go back to school with her friends. That you don't want to go home but she doesn't understand why."

Sitting back in her chair, Natalie considered the reasons she'd been using to avoid going back. "I know I should have stayed in Spring Lake for her. I just couldn't. It was too much. My parents are gone. Then losing my brother... I had nothing but pain there. I think running into my ex with his new girlfriend the day after the funeral sent me over the edge."

"How serious were you with him?"

"I thought he was going to propose the night we broke up. All of a sudden, everything I thought we had was gone. He took me to the restaurant where we had our first date. It never occurred to me he'd take me there to end things. My brother and his wife asked me to stay with them right after. They said they needed help looking after Shelly, but I think they just didn't want me to be alone."

"They sound like they were good people."

"They were the best." She swallowed against the emotion rising in her throat. "It wasn't fair of me to take Shelly away. And now this lunatic wants to kill her because I brought her here."

"No. He wants to kill her because he's a killer. That is nobody's fault but his. You can't let yourself take responsibility for what he's doing." Then he shook his head.

"What?"

"Well, here I am telling you the same thing my family has been telling me." He leaned back. "Guilt and regret won't change anything. All we can do is try to do our best as we move forward. All you've done is try your best to give Shelly what she needs."

"I worry it won't be enough. That I'm not enough."

This had been like an endless stream of thought for the last six months.

"From what I can see, you're more than enough. I have great parents, so I know what it looks like. I see it in you."

"Thank you for saying that. Will you tell me what happened to make people say these things to you? If you don't mind."

Rick's eyes drifted far away. He sat for a moment before he spoke. "I lost people overseas. It was supposed to be a fact-gathering mission. There weren't supposed to be any hostiles. My unit split up to do our parts. Everything was going as it should. Then, all at once, we were attacked. I lost half my team. People who trusted me to lead them. People who were too young to die. I know I must have missed something. Something that got my friends killed. I wasn't able to save them all." He slumped in the chair, his eyes downcast. "I tried. I wasn't fast enough."

Natalie leaned forward, her elbows on the table. "I don't know much about being in a war zone or running a military operation. I do know that sometimes bad things happen no matter how thoroughly we plan them out. Sometimes there are variables that are out of our control. All we can do is trust that God has a plan for us. It must have been hard for you when Shelly started talking about this."

He sat up quickly. "No. I think it helped me as much as it seemed to help her. Explaining things to her was so different than listening to other people try to tell me. Seeing things through her innocent eyes put everything into perspective. I didn't tell her much, but she tried to comfort me. She's an amazing kid."

Natalie couldn't help but smile. "She really is." She looked over at Shelly sleeping in the bed. She looked so peaceful. "You were really good with her tonight. You have no idea how much that means to me." She couldn't help but think that God had brought Rick into their lives for a reason. Maybe for more than his ability to protect them.

"I had been planning on leaving a couple weeks ago," Rick said. "Something kept me here. I think I was meant to be there when you came running through the woods last night. This is going to sound crazy but I feel as though God kept me here so I could help you. And maybe so Shelly could help me."

His words were so raw and honest. He clearly shared her faith and that endeared him to her even more. They were already thinking the same way about the things that mattered. It was another stark reminder of another piece that didn't fit with Eric. He believed in God, but not in a meaningful way. It was more of something in the background. He didn't pray or show any interest in reading the bible. He felt that he was the only one who knew what was best for him. He had always zoned out or changed the subject when Natalie suggested that he pray on things before making big decisions or entering into uncertain situations at work. How had she thought it would be a good idea to marry him? The more she thought about it, the more she realized they had nothing in common. More specifically, the core values that made Natalie who she was were completely different than the way her ex saw himself in the world.

Rick was everything she could want in a man. He was strong and kind. His faith guided him. He was great with children. Everything Eric hadn't been. It gave her hope that she might find the right person one day. That it was a blessing when her ex ended their relationship. He must have realized what she was only figuring out now.

As she and Rick continued to tell stories and ask questions of each other, they learned that they shared so many beliefs and interests. They even found themselves finishing each other's sentences a few times. It was beginning to feel as though they'd known each other for a long time. He told her about the company he'd built and that he had become restless. There was a security consulting job he was waiting to hear about in California. She hoped he would get it. He deserved happiness. There was no doubt he'd be good in that kind of position.

The thing that really struck her was how closely he listened when she spoke. The questions he asked pushed her to dig deeper. To open up to him. It was a little scary at first, but then it began to feel as natural as breathing. This was what it was supposed to be like. This was what she would look for in her next relationship. She was finally feeling a little hopeful for what the future could hold. For what God may have planned.

When they realized it was after three in the morning, they decided they should try to get some sleep. Rick checked on the officer outside. It wasn't the same one who had been there earlier. This one was a little older and had an alertness about him. It helped them feel comfortable going to sleep. It didn't take long before Natalie drifted off.

She found herself back in her brother's house surrounded by fire. She was frozen in place. Held there as if she wasn't supposed to leave. She could feel the heat. See the flames spread across the ceiling above. The one just below her brother's bedroom. She couldn't turn away. Couldn't see anything but the burning beams. It was twisting a knot in her stomach. But it wasn't fear. It wasn't the urgency to get Shelly out. For the first time, her niece wasn't there. Everything about it felt different. She just couldn't pinpoint what had changed. Only the flames remained the same, the smoke that filled her lungs. She began to gasp for breath, her mouth agape as she tried desperately to suck in oxygen that wasn't there. Then, suddenly, something shifted around her and she was pulled away.

Still gasping, with tears running down her face, she found herself back in the motel room.

Shelly was shaking Natalie's arm. Rick was standing over her. Was she crying out in her sleep? Did they know what she'd been dreaming about? Then she noticed Shelly's eyes were watery. Turning to Rick, she saw the strain in his features. Something was wrong. And it had nothing to do with her nightmares.

NINE

Natalie sat up quickly. "What's wrong?"

"Shelly's sick," Rick said. This was the last thing they needed. They'd have to take her to the doctor, risk putting her in danger again when he knew the prudent thing would be to stay put. "She feels pretty warm."

Natalie turned and put her hand on Shelly's forehead. "She's burning up. I need to get her to a doctor." She jumped out of bed and started digging in Shelly's duffel.

"We need to think carefully about how we'll do this." Rick stepped closer to Natalie.

She stopped and turned to him. He could see the reality of their situation sinking back in. Last night had been a nice distraction. It gave them a few hours to pretend that they weren't being hunted. That it wasn't about the need to keep Shelly hidden. Now, in the light of day, reality set back in.

"The police can take us." She grabbed an outfit for Shelly and brought it over to the bed. She helped her niece get changed. "He can't come after us if we're with a police officer."

"I think we should go without the police." When he saw her about to object, he put his hand up so she'd let him finish. "If we go with the police it'll draw attention.

And you know this guy won't hesitate just because a cop is with us." He didn't want to say anything specific that would scare Shelly. She didn't know about what happened to the officers who'd been posted outside their cottage. "Let's take a second to make a plan. I think we should go in my truck. Stay low-key. That way, no one takes notice and starts talking about it. The people here tell each other everything. They wouldn't have any way of knowing they shouldn't mention seeing us in a cop car. If we're in my truck, they're less likely to notice."

"What if the officer follows?"

"Yeah, no one would notice a cop following my truck all around town." He immediately regretted the sarcastic tone.

She grabbed clothes out of her duffel and started toward the bathroom. "Give me a minute to change. And to think." Then she closed the door.

Rick sat on the edge of the bed next to Shelly. "How're you doing, Peanut?"

"Not so good." She looked miserable.

"I know. We're going to bring you to the doctor. We'll get you fixed up."

Natalie came out looking more focused. "I called and made an appointment while I was changing. I don't think it'll make any difference. Based on what you're saying, I'm sure people have heard what happened. If anyone notices us, they're going to be talking about it whether a policeman is with us or not. I say we let the cops take us. It's safer to have them than not." She hesitated a second, then said, "Maybe I should just take her myself. You can wait here and—"

Rick stood up. "Absolutely not. I should be with you. Even with the police. If he shows up, how are you going to deal with him while taking care of Shelly?" When she didn't respond, he said, "Let me rephrase. I'd like to go with you. This guy doesn't seem to want to hurt me. And he feels very differently toward you and the police. Please let me do what I've been trained to do."

When Natalie nodded, relief flooded his body. She lifted Shelly into her arms, the child's head resting on her shoulder. "We need to go. The receptionist said we could bring her in now." Natalie moved quickly. She still had a limp but the adrenaline must have been fueling her movements. He could understand why.

Rick opened the door and found that Officer Hazel Clarke had taken over when the night shift ended. He told her what they needed to do. She didn't hesitate. Hazel made sure the motel room was locked up tight and then led them to her car. She opened the rear door of the cruiser and closed it once they were inside. Then she drove them into town. On the way, she made a call to have another officer sent to the motel to keep watch. She also requested officers be sent to meet them at the doctor's office to ensure their safety.

Even with all of these precautions, Rick didn't like being out in the open. He also considered that they could be followed back to the motel after the appointment. Or that they could be attacked at any point along the way to and from the center of town. Maybe even inside the doctor's office.

Driving through town didn't draw much attention. People were used to seeing the police around. It was when they arrived at the town doctor's office that people took notice. There were two other cruisers and four officers standing out front. This was exactly what he wanted to avoid. This was a spectacle. People would be talking.

Speculating. When they got out, two officers went around back to guard the rear door, while two stayed out front. Hazel came inside and waited with Rick in the hallway while Natalie went into the exam room with Shelly.

Rick considered what would happen if there was something seriously wrong with Shelly. They had no way to get her to a hospital with the bridge damaged. There was nowhere to safely land a helicopter to get them out. He would have suggested it yesterday if it was a viable option. Right now, all he could do was pray. *Please keep them safe. Please let Shelly be alright. Don't let anything happen to them. If someone has to be hurt, let it be me.*

The door opened and Natalie appeared with Shelly at her side. Her face was unreadable. Then she looked at him and smiled. "It's just an ear infection. He gave her something to bring the fever down. We have to pick up antibiotics at the pharmacy."

Thank You. His relief was visceral, and was spreading through him fast enough to nearly make him lightheaded. How had he come to care about Natalie and Shelly this much so quickly? He was determined to keep that from happening. He needed to stay focused. Clearheaded. Otherwise, he could make a mistake. One that might get them killed.

Hazel spoke up. "We'll escort you. It's a few doors down." She got on her radio and instructed the officers outside. Two were to go down and check the pharmacy and report back. The other two were to wait by the front door and be part of the escort. Rick couldn't deny that they were being thorough. That did nothing to ease his concern over how much attention this was going to draw.

The officers surrounded them. Hazel led in front, with one in the rear, one to the side. Rick took the other side.

They walked as quickly as Natalie could move with her injured foot. She was getting around better than he would have thought. Rick kept scanning faces, looking for anyone that fit the description. Anyone who looked at them with more than curiosity. Surely, everyone had heard about the incidents at his cabin and Natalie's cottage by now. Of course they would want a look at the woman and child at the center of all of this.

Jack McKenna was on the sidewalk across the street. He was watching them a little too intently. He was the perfect height and build. Jack owned a deli in town. Typically, it opened closer to lunchtime, so why was he roaming around town now? His short dark hair and deep brown eyes certainly fit what Shelly described. He wasn't the nicest of men, but was he capable of murder? He had the skills with a gun. Everyone in town knew his aim was stellar when he went hunting. Rick had no idea if he had the fighting skills. There'd never been a reason to find out. Rick kept his eye on Jack as they went inside the pharmacy. Two officers stayed outside. The others came in. Rick looked through the window. Jack was still watching.

Then he saw Tom Beckett stop out front and look in through the window. He was a teacher and a football coach at the high school. He had the build and the strength. The hair and eye color fit, too. Rick didn't like looking at people he'd known since he was a child as suspects, but he had no choice. When he saw Tom asking one of the officers a question, he wanted to go outside to hear what he was saying. The officers brushed him off and sent him on his way. Stopping across the street, not far from Jack, Tom turned and continued to watch them in the pharmacy. Rick had to remind himself that the people in Maple Rapids weren't used to seeing five police officers escorting and guarding people. Of course, they would ask questions and watch to see what was happening. It didn't mean they were guilty of anything.

Someone bumped into Rick from behind. He whirled around, ready for anything.

"Oh, hey there, Rick. Sorry. I'm just so late. I didn't mean to walk right into you that way." Dan Caraway stood before him. He'd seen Dan in Arnie's store the previous morning.

"It's okay. Is everything alright?"

"Oh, yeah. Everything's fine. I'm just late for an appointment. Sorry I can't stay and chat." He hurried out the door and up the street. Rick couldn't help but notice that Dan was a fit for the masked man, too. Not that he thought of Dan as someone capable of anything like that. He was one of the nicest people Rick had ever met. Sometimes a little too chatty, but that didn't make him a criminal.

"We're ready to go." Natalie came to Rick's side with Shelly next to her. "Once we get the antibiotics into her, she'll start getting better."

Rick nodded. "Good. Let's get back to the room. I don't like being out in the open like this." Rick scanned the street as they stepped outside.

"We need to get some food. She can't take this on an empty stomach."

Hazel spoke up. "Tell us what you'd like and I'll have it brought to the room. No sense in keeping you out here any longer than necessary."

Natalie was clearly uncomfortable. "I can't keep asking you guys to do everything for us." She looked at Rick, seeming to hope he'd agree. He couldn't. The best thing was to go back into hiding.

"It's no problem. Just tell me what to get and one of

these guys will bring it within the hour." Hazel smiled, trying to put her at ease. Natalie turned to Rick again.

"I get what you're feeling right now," he told her, "but we need to go. We're drawing too much attention." He saw it register in her eyes when she turned and saw Jack and Tom still staring at them. She nodded and began to walk back toward the police cars, with the five officers surrounding them. She told Hazel what they wanted to eat and got right into the back seat with Shelly. She was clearly a little rattled by the way they were being watched.

Rick took another quick scan of their surroundings. When he was about to get into the car, Henry Wilson came walking over from up the street. He was also a fit for the masked man. Rick didn't know where his money came from or what his skills were. He kept mostly to himself and never held a job in town. He didn't like how close Henry was getting.

Hazel stepped into his path. "Is there something you need, Henry?"

"I'm just wondering what's going on here. Who is that in the back of your car?" Henry was trying to get a look inside through the windshield.

Another officer stepped in his way. "Move along, please. This doesn't concern you, Mr. Wilson." His tone was filled with authority and warning.

Henry nodded and started walking away. His head kept swiveling back to see.

Rick got into the back seat next to Shelly and pulled the door closed. Hazel jumped in and drove much faster than she had during the ride into town. She kept checking the rearview mirror.

"This is why I didn't want the police involved," Rick said in a low voice to Natalie.

"It might have been worse without them."

"Or we might not have been noticed at all. This could have gone very wrong very quickly." He knew how to operate in a hostile environment without being seen. Natalie may not have understood that, but she was going to have to start trusting his instincts if she wanted to get through this alive.

She turned toward the window, pulling Shelly tighter against her side. Her breathing was faster than normal. She was clearly scared and trying not to let Shelly know. He shouldn't have said anything. He'd only made her more anxious.

When the car made a sudden sharp turn, Rick immediately turned to see if there was someone following them. Sure enough, there was a big blue pickup truck with tinted windows and chipped paint following a little too closely.

Hazel got on the radio. "I've got a pickup on my tail. I need backup now." She gave their location and hit the gas. If the officers didn't come quickly, things were going to get much worse.

Natalie turned to look out the rear window, fear clearly written all over her face. When the truck moved closer, nearly ramming the back bumper, she gasped and Shelly began to cry. If Rick had been the one to drive, he would have been able to outmaneuver the other driver. It was one of the many things he'd learned in his training. Hazel was young and fairly new to the force. She didn't have much experience. Rick had no doubt that she would grow into a fine officer with time. In this moment, though, she was still learning and lacked the evasive driving skills required. It was difficult for Rick to depend on anyone when Natalie and Shelly's lives were in jeopardy. Especially a rookie.

"Maybe I should drive." Rick leaned over the edge of the front seat.

"I don't see how you would do that right now," Hazel said.

"I'll climb over and switch with you."

"Rick, I know what you can do, but right now I need you to stay in your seat and let me focus on driving until backup comes."

A loud clap of metal colliding with metal ripped through the car as it jerked forward, having been rammed by the truck from behind. It began to turn toward the forest. The side windows were partially open, making the sound of the impact even louder. Hazel hit her head on the steering wheel and seemed a little dazed. Rick moved to take the wheel, reaching around from behind but Hazel was slumped over, making it impossible. They were careening toward a thick cluster of mature trees. Shelly's whimpers were hard to ignore but he had to get control of the car before they crashed.

"Hit the brakes! Hazel, hit the brakes!" Rick tried again to reach out for the steering wheel. They were seconds from impact.

TEN

Sirens blared in the distance as the police car came to a screeching halt. Rick was out of the car before Natalie could think to ask what he planned to do. She turned and watched through the rear window as a tall man with messy brown hair jumped down from inside the lifted pickup truck. He appeared to be muscular under a tattered pair of jeans and a gray-and-white flannel hanging open over a stained white T-shirt.

"You can't run from me!" He was coming fast. Rick immediately moved in front of him. "Get out of my way. She isn't getting away with this." The man tried to shove Rick but he stepped aside and grabbed the man's arm, twisting it in an awkward angle, forcing him to turn to the side. When the man realized he might be outmatched, he tried to step away. Rick reluctantly released him but stayed between the angry man and the mangled police car, where Natalie and Shelly were still sitting in the back seat. The man stared at Rick for a long moment and then turned back to the cruiser and yelled, "Get out of the car and face me!"

Hazel seemed to finally pull herself together after having hit her head, and she stumbled out of the car. There was a little blood trickling down her forehead and staining her blond hair. Natalie unhooked Shelly's seat belt and eased her down to the floor. Continuing to watch through the rear window, she tried to keep low in case the man had a gun.

"You clearly want to go to jail, Ray. Rick, please step aside." Hazel's tone was authoritative. Her posture was straight and she seemed to move with purpose. "Ray, you need to turn around and lean against the side of your truck. You know the drill." She pulled her gun from the holster and pointed it at the man she called Ray.

Three police cars pulled up. Officer Dennis ran to Rick and they came together back to the car, where Natalie and Shelly were waiting. There was a lot of commotion after that. Officers yelling. Ray trying to push his way toward Hazel. He wasn't going to go down without a fight. When they finally got him cuffed, they tried to put him into the back of another cruiser. Hazel read him his rights as the other officers dealt with his resistance. Given the amount of blood trickling down the side of her face, it was surprising she was still involved at all. She didn't hesitate to jump in when Ray was getting the better of one of the other officers.

Once everything was calm, Officer Dennis opened the car door and leaned in. "This isn't our guy. This is something unrelated. He has a grudge with Hazel. She arrested him a few times. Everything is under control. We still have every reason to believe your location is unknown."

"You can get up now." Natalie pulled Shelly into her arms. She didn't like that her niece had endured another violent episode. How much more would the child have to deal with before this was finally over? "What do we do now?" Natalie asked as she looked back and forth between Rick and Officer Dennis.

Rick turned to Pete Dennis. "We've been here too long. We need to get moving."

"I'll have another officer bring you back to the motel and take the day shift. I want Hazel to get checked out." Officer Dennis turned and waved over one of the other officers. He jogged quickly to Pete's side. "This is Officer Lee Kramer," Pete told Natalie. "He'll be taking over and getting you back to your room. He'll stay until someone relieves him to take the night watch." He looked down at Shelly in Natalie's arms. "I heard she wasn't feeling well. How's she doing?"

Rick spoke up. He had been watching everything very closely. "She has an ear infection. We got meds in town. We need to get her back to bed. And she should eat something. Do you think the food will be there when we get back?" Rick's tone conveyed his need to protect them. Natalie appreciated that he was there with them. It was foolish to have suggested that he stay behind today. Maybe she should have listened to him when he said they should go alone. Ray wouldn't have tried to run them off the road. Rick had been right about how much attention the police presence had drawn. People had stood around watching. Some had seemed to put Rick on edge. It was entirely possible that the killer was standing right in front of them in town. The thought of it sent a shiver through her body.

Officer Dennis nodded. "Food's on the way. It should be there by the time you get back."

"Let's get going then. I don't like being out here. This guy could've heard about this and could be on his way to shoot from somewhere in the woods. We know he's a good shot." Rick seemed impatient. Natalie was feeling a similar sense of urgency. Waiting in that crumpled car while that man tried to attack Hazel was wearing Natalie's nerves thin. Anything could have happened. It was difficult to live in this constant uncertainty. She couldn't help but wonder if this was somehow part of God's plan. If it was, Natalie was having a difficult time understanding what good could possibly come from any of this.

Officer Dennis stepped away and spoke to Lee Kramer and Rick, then told them he'd stop in to give them an update in a few hours.

Officer Kramer came to the door and leaned down. "We need to move you to another vehicle."

More officers, including Pete Dennis, came over and surrounded them as they got out and walked about fifteen yards toward another car. They had all stopped behind the truck that had rammed Hazel's police car. Rick stayed close to them, inside the circle of police. Officer Kramer led the way. He was as tall as Rick with a similar athletic physique. His hair was buzzed close to his head.

It was a strange thing to fear being outside. To feel so exposed and uncertain of what could happen next just walking down the street. Getting outside had been her escape in recent months. Now, she didn't even have that. Natalie's heart was racing. Her mouth felt dry. She kept gripping Shelly tighter against her. Instinctively, Natalie slouched down in an attempt to keep her niece hidden behind the men surrounding them.

Shelly wiggled in Natalie's arms. "I can walk." She shifted her weight so Natalie would let her down. Maybe that was better. She wouldn't be as easy to see.

Just as Natalie bent down to put Shelly on her feet, one of the officers fell to the pavement next to her. Blood was soaking through his uniform sleeve. Rick grabbed Shelly into his arms and pressed her against Natalie from behind, wrapping himself around both of them. He hurried them into the car as Officer Kramer jumped into the driver's seat. That was too close. What if Shelly hadn't moved in that moment? Would the bullet have hit one of them?

"Get in and get low." Rick's voice sliced into Natalie's ear. As she did what he said, he blanketed himself over them after pulling the door closed. Officer Kramer sped off immediately. A shot hit the rear-side window. Glass exploded into the car. Tiny shards hit the floor around Natalie's head. She tried to spread her body over Shelly to make sure every part of her was covered. She felt Rick doing the same thing above her.

"Are you okay?" Rick's voice was urgent. "Are either of you hit?"

Natalie shook her head. "No, we're good. Just some glass."

The car lurched around corners and propelled forward out of every turn. "I'm just making sure we're clear before returning to the motel. I don't want anyone to be able to follow," Officer Kramer said. "I think you can get up now. If he was in the woods shooting, it's unlikely he could get to a car to pursue us before we get out of range. This will give Pete and the others a chance to apprehend him. Given who got hit, they'll know the general direction to start looking."

Rick eased off and brushed the bits of glass to one side before helping Natalie, then Shelly, into the seat. He pulled the seat belt around Shelly and clicked it into place. Then he pushed the glass off the seat and sat down.

"You think it's him? You don't think it might be one of Ray's buddies trying to back him up?" Rick was looking at Officer Kramer in the rearview mirror.

"I suppose we'll find out when they catch whoever

took the shot." The policeman didn't seem interested in speculation.

When they pulled into the motel parking lot, two officers came over to the car and escorted them to the room, again with Officer Kramer leading the way. It was pretty quiet there. Given that there were only a few other cars scattered in front of other rooms, it seemed like most of the visitors had already checked out. No one was outside. The only sounds came from the breeze blowing through the leaves and the birds singing from within the trees. It would have been peaceful if there wasn't so much adrenaline coursing through Natalie's veins.

The sound of a crack had the officers stopping and drawing their guns. Rick moved closer, his arms wrapping around Natalie, his head turning in every direction. Shelly's eyes were wide with fear. Another crack brought their guns around to one direction. What was coming now?

It was impossible to be sure where the noise was coming from and what may have been causing it, given the way the sound bounced off the building and echoed through the trees. Rick started edging Natalie and Shelly forward. Standing in the middle of the parking lot made them easy targets.

"We need to get them inside before whoever that is makes a move." He spoke to Lee, knowing he was experienced. When Lee nodded, they continued forward, their feet crunching through the gravel until they reached the steps to the porch that ran along the front side of the motel. Lee came inside with them while the other officers stayed outside to assess the situation or neutralize a potential shooter.

Rick noticed the bags of food sitting on the small table where they'd played cards the night before. If felt like a week since they'd been in the room, not the few hours it had actually been. He watched as Natalie brought Shelly into the bathroom and got down low inside the tub. It was smart thinking. If someone opened fire, they wouldn't get hit unless the bullets came from above.

Rick closed the door and then stood in front of it while Lee remained in the middle of the room. He seemed focused, listening for sounds from outside.

A sudden rap on the door had Lee moving to look through the window. He quickly stepped outside, pulling the door closed behind him. Rick walked to the front window and saw him talking to the other officers. A moment later, Lee came back inside and the others headed across the parking lot.

"It was a bear," Lee explained. "He was trying to climb up a tree and the branches broke. The bear nearly fell on top of them while they were looking. I'll be outside the door. Don't hesitate to call for me if you need something." When Rick nodded, Lee stepped outside and pulled the door closed.

Rick knocked on the bathroom door. "You can come out now. It's all clear."

The door opened and Shelly stepped through first. "I'm starving."

Natalie walked her over to the table and started pulling containers out of the bags. She put the chicken noodle soup in front of Shelly and handed her a spoon. "How are you feeling?" Natalie pressed her hand to Shelly's forehead and then on the back of her neck. "Once you're done eating your soup and chicken fingers, I'll give you the medicine."

"Thanks, Aunt Natty. The soup is good. Are you guys eating with me?" Shelly turned to look at Rick.

"Of course." He took the seat next to her. Natalie sat on the other side of the table. He paused before opening the container Natalie put in front of him to say a prayer. To thank God for getting them back to the motel safely. He saw Natalie watching him. "Just giving thanks."

She smiled and nodded, then turned to Shelly. "I think you should get back in bed after you eat. You need rest so your body can work on making you better."

"You said we would play cards again today. I don't want to go to bed." Shelly pushed away her soup.

"I did say that, but I didn't know you would be sick. How about if we play for a half hour and then you take a nap? If you're feeling better when you wake up, we'll play again."

"I guess. I'll get the cards." Shelly was about to get up when Natalie put her hand on Shelly's shoulder.

"Why don't we finish eating first? Then we'll play." Natalie gave her a small grin.

Rick couldn't imagine how they were holding up so well. When they finished the meal and Shelly took the pink liquid the doctor prescribed, she bounded out of her seat to get the cards. She wasn't as lively as she'd been the night before, but she was definitely working hard to create a new game. The rules kept changing. Shelly's eyebrows pulled together as she concentrated on new ways to use the cards. It wasn't long before her energy seemed to fade. Then Natalie decided it was time for her to get back in bed.

Using an ear thermometer they picked up in the pharmacy, Natalie took Shelly's temperature. "You're down to ninety-nine-point-eight. Much better than earlier. Get some rest." She pulled the blanket up to Shelly's chin and kissed her forehead. "Sweet dreams." With the curtains closed, the room wasn't very bright. Being tucked into a dense patch of trees certainly didn't help let the sunlight brighten this place. It was easily dark enough for a nap. It wasn't long before Shelly's soft snores confirmed she had dozed off.

Rick could live with the dreariness of the place if it meant the assailant wouldn't be able to find them. That Natalie and Shelly would be safe there. In his gut, he knew there was no such place. A man like that would find a way. He would keep coming until he finished what he started.

ELEVEN

As the hours went by and night fell with no word from Officer Dennis, it began to feel like this would never end. Natalie had tried everything to distract herself. At least Shelly was beginning to feel a little better. Rick had been taking regular walks around the perimeter of the motel to make sure no one was lurking around. A knock on the door put a halt to the card game Shelly was playing with them. Rick stood up and moved quietly to the door. That's when Officer Lee Kramer spoke up.

"It's Lee. Pete just pulled in. I'm sure he'll be wanting to come in and check on you." Lee stepped aside when Rick opened the door. Pete Dennis came up the few stairs, onto the porch and into the room.

"Did you catch him?" Natalie stood up, anxious for any kind of good news.

Rick pushed the door closed behind him. "Was it him?"

"Well, we caught the shooter. It was one of Ray's cousins. He was out there hunting and saw the commotion. He thought it was Ray in the huddle and in the car. He was probably looking at his phone when Ray was put in a different car. He's not very bright." Officer Dennis sighed in what seemed to be a mix of frustration and exhaustion. Natalie wondered if he'd slept yet.

What that told her was that they were stuck there for the foreseeable future. It didn't sit well. This town seemed to suddenly be coming apart at the seams. "Is it possible to get out of town yet? I don't feel like we would be safe anywhere in the area."

Officer Dennis nodded. "I understand that. Unfortunately, there isn't a safe way out yet." He looked at Shelly and then turned to Rick. "Let's go outside for a minute."

Natalie spoke up before they could leave. "Officer Dennis, how long do you think it'll take to fix the bridge?"

"Please call me Pete. I'm sorry but that'll be at least a week. If the river calms down, I'll get you out by boat. Until then, I'm afraid you'll have to stay put." She could hear the regret in his voice.

"I'll be right back." Rick followed him outside.

Natalie stood staring at the door. She could feel the anxiety spilling through her body. Her breaths were becoming shallow and quick. Every minute they were stuck here was another opportunity for the killer to find them and finish what he started. She was beginning to feel trapped. The room was so small and dark. The lighting was dim at best. She needed to get outside. To breathe fresh air. To be able to sleep without waking to every little noise.

"Aunt Natty?" Shelly brought Natalie's attention back to the room. She had to hold it together. Keeping Shelly calm took precedence over her own fears.

As she turned, she adjusted her expression, wiping the tension away. "What is it, sweetie? Are you hungry?"

"No. I'm still full from dinner. I was wondering if we can go home when the bridge is fixed? I mean our real home."

"That's the plan. The minute we can go, we'll head

home." Natalie was feeling just as eager to get back to Spring Lake as Shelly was. The feel of the ocean breeze would be a welcome change.

"Can I go back to my school? With my friends?"

"Yes, if it's what you want."

Shelly nodded her head. "I do." She seemed to be thinking about something. Her eyebrows pulled together a little. "Are we safe here?"

Natalie didn't know how to answer that. She had no idea. She didn't want to lie but she didn't want to cause Shelly any unnecessary stress. "We are right now. There are two policemen outside. Rick is here. They will do everything they can to keep us safe."

Shelly thought about that statement for a moment. This was so much for her niece to have to process at such a young age. "Is Rick coming home with us when the bridge is fixed?"

That question took Natalie by surprise. "I don't think so, honey. It's so nice that he's helping us here, but he has his own life to get back to. It wouldn't be fair to expect that of him, would it?"

Shelly's gaze fell to the floor. "I guess not."

"You like him a lot, huh?" Natalie felt some of the same disappointment at the prospect of not seeing Rick anymore. It wasn't just that he'd been willing to put himself in harm's way to protect them. There was so much more to him. His values. The comfort in having so many things in common. She'd never had that with someone outside her family before. At least now, she knew that it was possible to find people like him. Although, she didn't imagine there were many.

Shelly shrugged her shoulders. The last thing Natalie

wanted was for her niece to become attached to someone who would eventually leave.

"Rick will always be our friend," Natalie told her. "Maybe we can invite him to visit some time." She wasn't sure he'd be interested in coming but she wouldn't mind being able to see him again. He was a good man. The kind you don't find very often. Someone she could see having as a good friend.

Shelly perked up. "Can I ask him?"

"I think that would be a great idea. But let's wait until it's time to go home. Let's not put him on the spot now, okay?"

As Shelly nodded, the door opened and Rick came back inside. His expression was grim, making Natalie's stomach drop. She knew she couldn't ask him what he found out until Shelly went to sleep. Given his expression, it was clear the news wasn't good.

Rick smiled at Shelly and rubbed his hands together. "Who's ready for a new game?"

The girl's eyes widened with excitement. "What game?"

A knock at the door had Rick pulling it open. Pete came in carrying a stack of board games with a grocery bag on top. He set it all down on the table.

"I brought some things to help you pass the time." He opened the grocery bag and held it low for Shelly to see. "And I brought snacks."

Shelly looked inside the bag. "Can I take some?"

"Of course. That's why I brought 'em." Pete's smile didn't reach his eyes. At least he was trying to hide whatever he knew from Shelly. Natalie appreciated that. Once she picked the snack she wanted, Pete put the bag on the table. "I need to get going. Don't hesitate to call if you need anything or if something feels off. I don't care what time it is."

"I appreciate that. And thank you for bringing all of this." Natalie gestured toward the games and snacks.

"No problem." He turned to Shelly. "I'll see you tomorrow morning, young lady. What would you like for breakfast?"

Shelly couldn't contain her smile. She pressed her finger to her chin. "Hmm. Maybe…French toast."

"You got it. I'll see you all in the morning. Try and get some rest."

"Thanks, Pete. Let me know if you hear anything else." Rick walked him outside.

"Will do." Pete jogged down the few stairs to the gravel parking lot and got into his car. Natalie watched through the open door and saw Pete lift his radio close to his mouth through the car window. A moment later, he pulled out in a hurry. Once he was down the road, his lights came on. Something must have happened in another part of town.

Natalie stepped out onto the porch and took in a deep breath of the cool night air. It was barely a moment before Officer Kramer was gesturing for them to go back inside. She understood why. It was just frustrating to think that this criminal could wield so much power over all of them. She was looking forward to him being locked away.

Rick initiated a game of *Trouble* and didn't seem to have any difficulty pretending that this was all normal. The good thing about it was that it helped Shelly forget she was in danger. She laughed and bossed him around like she had the night before. It was nice to see her having fun. It would help keep her mind off what was actually happening.

When a text came in on Rick's phone, Natalie saw the

name *Pete Dennis* pop up on the screen. He stepped away from the table to open it. Once he was finished reading what it said, his eyes flashed with tension. He looked at Natalie for a moment, then put the phone in his back pocket and sat back down at the table to continue the game with Shelly. He kept up the silly talk but she could see the new tension in his shoulders. It made her wonder what Pete had told him in that text. What new problem was coming their way? She still didn't know what Pete had told Rick earlier. Now, something else was happening.

Natalie stood up and looked out the front window to see Officer Kramer still sitting out there. It made her wonder why someone hadn't come to relieve him yet. Where were the other officers? What was happening that kept Pete from sending someone to take over for the overnight shift? She closed her eyes and began to pray.

Watching Natalie put Shelly to bed, tucking her under the covers, gave Rick a sense of peace he hadn't felt in many years. It was almost as if they were a family on vacation.

"Good night, Rick," Shelly called over to him.

He walked over to the side of the bed, next to Natalie. "Good night, Peanut." When she reached her arms out, Rick bent over to hug her. She wrapped her arms around his neck, pulling him closer.

"Can we play another one of the games tomorrow?" She released his neck and looked up at him with those big chocolate-brown eyes. Who could resist her?

"Of course, we can." He kissed her forehead. "Get some rest."

Shelly nodded and curled in under the blanket. Rick stood with Natalie watching her as she dozed off. It was in that moment that he realized that the restlessness was gone. He hadn't felt it while he was with Natalie and Shelly. There was a kind of peace being there with them. He considered that it could be that he was preoccupied with the situation and that he was always good in a fight, but that didn't track. He enjoyed playing the games with them. The banter with Shelly. The deeper conversations with Natalie. This was what had been missing from his life. He knew he wanted a family one day, much like the one he'd grown up in. He just hadn't thought about it in a while. He was always close with his parents and his sister. He had a great relationship with his brother-in-law. He glanced at Natalie. She was one of the most beautiful women he'd ever seen. Those warm brown eyes. That thick curly hair. The kindness in her face. He wanted someone like her. Someone who made him feel whole. Someone who listened when he spoke the way she did. Someone who shared his beliefs and codes of conduct.

Natalie nodded her head sideways and walked over to the table. Rick followed.

"What's going on? What did Pete tell you earlier? And the text?" Natalie's whisper held some anxiety.

Rick glanced back toward Shelly to make sure she was really sleeping. Then he turned to Natalie and spoke in a whisper. "They got the warrants for the shooting range. The owner didn't let the police take the casings or the security camera footage without one. Not that Pete's overly optimistic about getting anything useful there. I think he's just covering as many angles as possible. They're running checks on some guys in town. Pete is sick over it. He already cleared five but there are still nine more."

Natalie watched him, waiting for more. "Keep going. I know that isn't all of it." He could see her mind at work.

He really did want someone like her. She was intelligent, on top of all of her other attributes.

"There were a few break-ins in town, a couple businesses, some cars vandalized, the windows smashed out in a cop's house." He saw her eyes widen. "The cops are busy. It's why Lee is still here. He won't be relieved until one of the others can come."

"What else?"

"The text earlier? That was Pete. He said Arnie's place was hit. It's the general store in town. The front windows were shot out with people inside." He hesitated but when Natalie looked at him expectantly, he continued. "Pete thinks this might be the shooter trying to keep the cops busy so he can make a move. He doesn't believe the guy could know where we are but he warned me to stay vigilant."

"Anything else?"

"That's everything he told me. He was letting me know because Lee has been here since this morning. He'll be getting tired. He refused to leave, which is good, but Pete wanted me to keep watch, too."

Natalie nodded as she took a seat at the table. Rick sat across from her and reached out, taking her hands in his. "I won't let anything happen to either of you. I will do whatever it takes. You believe that, right?" Her hands were so soft and warm. They tucked perfectly into his. When she looked up at him, there was something there. It felt like a connection. Then she gripped the tips of his fingers a little tighter.

"I believe you'll put yourself in danger to protect us. It doesn't guarantee anything. And I don't like the idea of you getting hurt for us. Or worse." She was right. He couldn't give absolutes. "All we can do is wait." She paused, then asked, "Would you want to pray with me?"

He tightened his hands around hers. "I would really like that."

She spoke first. She thanked God for bringing Rick into her and Shelly's lives and asked that he be kept from harm. She thanked Him for the help from the police. She was full of so much gratitude rather than being angry for what was happening. When she was finished, he continued the prayer. He spoke for the people he'd lost and gave thanks for the ones who had survived. He also asked God to keep Natalie and Shelly safe. To give him what he needed to protect them.

When Rick opened his eyes, Natalie was watching him with a kind of warmth that made him wish they could have met under different circumstances. Being here with her, even in this situation, he felt more grounded. More connected. Maybe it was because he had a sense of purpose again. Maybe, because of his background, he needed the adrenaline rush. When he really thought about it, he hadn't missed that part of his life at all since coming home. He actually preferred the calm of everyday life. No. He believed it was being with Natalie and Shelly. The way they filled him with things he never thought he'd have the privilege of feeling. At least now, he knew it was a possibility for him. He imagined Natalie wouldn't want to see him again when this was over. Why would she ever want to be reminded of what happened here?

Natalie's soft voice interrupted his thoughts. "Do you think you'd still be in the Special Forces if that mission hadn't gone wrong?"

"I don't think so. I was getting to the point that I was ready to leave. I was beginning to feel like I had given what I could and wanted less action. I like to feel as though I'm contributing something but I was ready for a less intense way to go about it. How about you? What are you looking for?"

"I definitely don't want any more of what we've been dealing with here. The most important thing is providing stability for Shelly. I guess I want what my parents had. What my brother and his wife had. I want to be able to share my life with a person who I feel safe enough with to be who I really am. Does that make sense?"

"It makes perfect sense." He was about to say more when Natalie yawned. As much as he wanted to continue talking, he knew he needed to focus on the real reason he was there. "You should get some sleep. I'm going out to do a quick sweep. I'll keep watch until someone comes to relieve Lee."

"I can keep you company. You shouldn't have to stay awake alone." Her big brown sleepy eyes blinked with those long lashes sweeping lazily over her skin.

"Shelly will need you to be at your best in the morning. I'm used to functioning for long periods of time without sleep."

"If you need company, will you wake me up?"

"If I find myself having a difficult time staying awake, I'll get you up to keep me company. For now, get some rest." He got up and walked toward the door. "I'll be right back." When she nodded, he went outside.

Lee turned toward him. The poor guy looked exhausted. "Do you guys need anything in there?"

Rick shook his head. "I figured I'd do a quick perimeter sweep. Are they going to send someone to relieve you soon?"

"Eventually. Pete told you what's going on in town, right?"

"He did. I agree that it's probably a diversion. Try to keep sharp. I'll be staying up tonight to help keep watch." When Lee nodded, Rick walked down the steps and around the back of the motel. He moved slowly and tried to keep his steps quiet. He focused on the sounds around him. Everything seemed to be as it should. Typical night critters. No unusual movement.

He stood behind their room and looked up at the window. He didn't think he could easily jump up and get through without something to stand on. It wouldn't be a problem to jump down, though. That was something he wanted to check out in case the need arose. He kept moving along the rear of the motel. He could see the shifting light of televisions from two of the rooms. He would have preferred a place that didn't involve other people if this guy found them. He fully intended on discussing it with Pete in the morning. There was too much going on in town to trouble his old friend with that now.

When he came around to the front, at the other end, he saw that Lee's chair was empty. He scanned across all of the rooms. No one was there. He glanced over at the police car. Empty. Rick started running toward the room. Where was Lee? Had the killer come while Rick was walking around back? Was he inside the room with Natalie and Shelly right now?

TWELVE

The door slammed open into the wall. Natalie's entire body jolted from the suddenness of it. She quickly shifted herself close to Shelly. Rick stepped through the door, looking wild-eyed. His gaze was darting everywhere so quickly.

"What's wrong? Did something happen?" Natalie's heart was thumping so hard it felt as though it might break through her chest.

When his eyes landed on Officer Kramer, he seemed to calm down. "When I saw your chair empty and you were nowhere in sight, I thought…" He was talking to the officer.

"Sorry. I just needed a little something to pick me up. I knew Pete brought soda and snacks earlier. I was coming right back out." Lee started walking toward the door.

Natalie spoke up. "He asked me to bring something out. I told him to come in for a minute. I thought it would be good for him to get up and move around. I knew you were outside. That you'd know if someone was approaching." She felt bad. She hadn't intended to cause worry.

"I'm just glad that's all it is." Rick stepped aside as Lee passed through the door. "Let me know if you need anything else. Pete brought plenty."

"This is great for now. Thanks." Lee pulled the door closed behind him.

The noise had woken Shelly. She sat up in bed. "Is it morning?"

Rick came over to her bedside, next to Natalie. "No, Peanut. Lee was just a little hungry. You can go back to sleep."

Shelly wasn't quite awake. It didn't take long for her to doze off again. Rick turned off the lights and took a seat at the table. Natalie was about to join him when his low voice broke the silence.

"Get some sleep. I'm wide-awake after that. I plan to talk to Pete about moving us in the morning. I don't think we should stay anywhere too long. And I don't like the idea of others being around if something happens. You can take the other bed if you want. I won't be using it tonight."

Natalie sat on the edge of Rick's bed. "Are you sure? We could take turns."

"I've been coming to this town most of my life. I know the rhythms of the night here. I'll know if something is off. You can be sure I'll wake you up if we need to move." He stood up and went to the back window. Then the front. His movements were very quiet.

Natalie couldn't deny she was tired. She pulled the blankets back, kicked her shoes off and climbed under. "If you start to feel like you need a break, wake me up. I'm used to being awake at night, too."

Rick nodded and then went back to checking through the windows. He didn't seem interested in talking. There was an intensity about him now. He had become more closed off. She had noticed this with him at times. She wasn't sure if it was part of the way he functioned when he needed to be alert, or if it was his way of trying to keep

Natalie from getting too close to him. That would make sense since they weren't likely to cross paths again after this was over. Natalie couldn't imagine coming back to Maple Rapids again. There was also the fact that Rick would very likely be moving to California for that job he was waiting to hear about. The idea of not seeing him again was more disappointing than it should be. They barely knew each other. Even though it didn't feel that way, that was the truth of it. No point in expecting more. He was clearly intent on keeping his distance. His being nice to Shelly shouldn't have given her any expectations. Rick was going above and beyond for them.

Natalie closed her eyes and tried to be still. With Shelly sick and the possibility of being moved in the morning, rest made sense. It took some time, but she finally drifted off. It was that kind of sleep that let her clutch to consciousness at the same time. She was aware of Rick's movements and the sound of an owl outside. Fear made it difficult to fully let go. Her mind put her on the sand, close to the ocean. The lazy waves rolled in and out as Shelly made a sandcastle. Then a familiar smell had her turning toward the houses across the street from the boardwalk. Her heart began to pound in her chest. What was it? She turned and saw Shelly standing in the sand. It was as if she was screaming but no sound was coming out. What was that smell? Her mind twisted with panic. Shelly's mouth was wide open. Her chest was heaving with effort. Still no sound.

Then she was shaken awake. A loud beeping was lashing her ears. Smoke. The smell was smoke. Natalie jumped out of bed. She was reaching for Shelly when she realized Rick already had her in his arms. Delirium made it difficult to focus.

"We have to go!" Rick yelled. "Can you hear me? Natalie! We have to go through the window." He pushed on the frame and opened it.

There was a fire. Another fire. Natalie glanced toward the entrance and saw thick smoke coming through the cracks between the edges of the door and the frame. It was right outside. It was coming for them. How could this be happening again? Her body tensed with an almost paralyzing fear. It didn't seem possible that they could get through this twice in less than a year. She thought of Shelly. She was everything to Natalie. Because of her, Natalie knew there was no choice but to fight through it. Again. She turned and ran to the window, ready to do whatever it took to keep her niece alive.

Rick handed Shelly off to her. "I'm going to jump down. You can lower her to me. Then I'll help you. Can you do this?" He waited for her to respond.

"Yes. Go. Let's get her out of here." Natalie held Shelly close. The smoke was filling the room. Flames began to wrap around the door and spread across the front wall. They were running out of time.

Rick called to her a moment later. Natalie tried to push Shelly through the window but she was clinging to Natalie's neck.

"You have to let go. I'll be right behind you."

"No! Come with me!" Shelly was terrified, her voice cracking under the tears.

"I will but we can't fit together. And Rick can only take one of us at a time. I'll come right after you. I promise."

Natalie unclasped Shelly's hands from her neck and lowered her down to Rick. She was about to climb through the window when a crack from the fire turned her around. She could hear screaming but knew it wasn't here in the room. She froze. Her head began to spin. Her vision blurred. She was barely breathing. The screams were in her head and she knew exactly where they were coming from. It was the sound of her sister-in-law. She had been screaming that night. It had barely been audible over the roar of the growing fire and Shelly calling from the stairs. The panic alone had kept Natalie from thinking clearly that night. The only thing that she had been able to focus on was getting her niece to safety.

This was what had been bringing her back to that night in her dreams. Shelly's parents hadn't died in their sleep without suffering, as Natalie had believed. The thought of it nearly brought her to her knees in the middle of the smoke and flames engulfing the room. The realization that her brother and his wife had suffered in those last moments brought tears to her eyes. Their faces flashed in her mind. Who they were. Everything they'd done for her. Her heart was breaking all over again.

The sound of Rick and Shelly calling to her brought Natalie's head back into the present. Her lungs felt tight. The air was thinning. She had to get out. Fast. She grasped the window casing when the door suddenly slammed open. She expected to see Lee Kramer or another officer. Instead, the masked man burst through the flames and into the room. He let the thick blanket that had been wrapped around him drop to the floor, the flames sliding over it as it fell. Natalie immediately started climbing out the window. Rick was waiting below with Shelly close to his side. Just as she was dangling above the ground, about to let go of the window frame, the masked man grabbed one of her wrists. He was pulling her up as Rick was trying to get ahold of her legs. She struggled, pushing with her free hand against the outside wall while trying to pull free from the killer's grip. It was useless. He was too strong. She felt her body being lifted back in through the window.

Shelly was crying, calling her name. Rick must have felt so conflicted being stuck there with her niece while the killer was dragging her back into the fire. He couldn't leave Shelly to help her. At least, she hoped he wouldn't.

When her waist hit the windowsill, she reached up and grabbed ahold of the fabric covering the assailant's face. If she was going to die, she wanted to see the face of the man who was about to take her life. Maybe she'd recognize him and be able to call out his name before he silenced her.

The mask was slowly sliding over his head. Her grip was awkward, making her effort slow. Just as it was about to slip over his hairline, he released her wrist and grabbed the mask with both hands. She immediately fell back through the window, scraping her ribs on something as she fell. She kept watching to see if she could get a glimpse of the killer's face. Then she realized she was going to hit the ground without preparing for the landing. She shifted her gaze to look down just as she landed in Rick's arms. He pulled her against his chest, wrapping her in a tight embrace.

"Don't scare me like that." He set her down. "Can you run?"

Shelly threw her arms around Natalie's hips. She nodded toward Rick as she rubbed her niece's back. "I'll be fine. He'll be coming. We need to go now." She turned back toward the room. The masked man wasn't watching through the window. Which meant he was probably already making his way outside to come around to where they were. At least the fire would slow him down a little.

She couldn't help but wonder what had happened to the officer out front. Was it Lee or someone else that had come to take his place sometime in the night? Was that officer alright? She said a prayer for him or her as she turned back to Rick and Shelly. The structure of the motel was beginning to come apart. The sounds were more familiar than she would have liked. But she wouldn't let it paralyze her anymore.

Rick swooped Shelly into his arms and began to run. He kept glancing back to see that Natalie was following. She stayed close, just as eager as he was to put distance between them and the burning motel. The killer wouldn't be far behind.

The forest was eerily quiet except for their footsteps and the groans of the motel as it was coming apart. This silence was what had initially alerted Rick that something was wrong back in the room. He had dozed off in the chair but the lack of sound woke him. When he got up to look out the window he noticed smoke coming through the cracks in the door. Before he had the chance to open it, the fire alarm started blaring and then he saw the first hints of flames edging under the door. After that, he became focused on getting Natalie and Shelly out before it was too late.

He shook off the memory and listened to each crack and break of the structure as they echoed through the forest. Now that they had gotten some distance from the motel he realized that morning would be coming soon. The sun hadn't quite lifted over the horizon yet. It wasn't fully dark anymore, but it wasn't as easy to see as he would have liked.

When the sound of sirens finally could be heard in the

distance, moving closer as they ran for their lives, Rick considered going back so the police could help him protect Natalie and her niece. Then he thought better of it. The killer could be anywhere. Going back could put them right in his sights. It would have been ideal if they could have at least taken Rick's truck. They hadn't even been able to take any of their belongings. There hadn't been any time and it wasn't exactly what he'd thought about in that moment. There was nothing to do now but keep going. Rick hoped no one was hurt. At least there weren't very many people staying in the motel. He sent up a silent prayer. *Please don't let anyone get hurt in the fire. Help us find a safe way out of this.*

It wasn't long before Rick could make out the sound of someone else running, interrupting his thoughts in prayer. The snapping of twigs and the crunching of dead leaves on the forest floor pushed him to run faster. He turned and realized Natalie was beginning to fall behind. She was clutching her ribs on one side. She must have been injured when the killer was pulling her back inside. How much longer could she keep going? If they stopped, it wouldn't be long before the man pursuing them caught up. And he was very good with a gun.

He stopped to wait for Natalie. He had to figure out where to go and fast. Natalie was clearly injured and Shelly was sick. Neither of them could run very far. Then he remembered a hunting shed some of the guys in town kept nearby. They stored a few quads there, along with some first-aid supplies for emergencies. It wasn't far from where they were.

When Natalie caught up, he had her stop so he could listen to figure out how close the killer was getting to them. Natalie was out of breath. He worried how badly she was hurt. He would deal with that later. As long as she could keep moving, they'd continue to run.

"There's a shed near here that might have quads we can borrow. It'll get us out of his range so we can figure out what to do. Can you keep going?"

She nodded. "Lead the way."

"Are you sure? I can carry you on my back."

"Focus on Shelly. She's the priority. I'll keep up." Natalie looked down at Shelly, who was tucked in his arms, and kissed her forehead. Then her expression became very intense as her eyes met his. "Don't wait for me if I fall behind. Get her to safety." He tried to interrupt. "We don't have time to debate this. I'm asking you to put her life before mine. Can I count on you to do that?"

Taking a breath, Rick nodded. There was no time to argue and he understood why she felt this way. "I can. But please try to keep up." He turned and started jogging. Not as fast as he could be going, but he wanted Natalie to have a chance. Their pursuer was far enough behind them that he felt they could get to the shed in time moving at a slower pace. He just hoped the quads were still there.

He couldn't help but turn back to check that Natalie was still with him as he moved through the dark trees. The noise of each step made it easy for the masked man to track them even though he couldn't yet see them. Shelly clutched his neck, her head tucked against his chest. She felt so fragile to him in that moment. The idea of anything happening to either her or Natalie would be too much. He couldn't fail this time.

A hint of morning light cast a faint glow around the wood shed fifty yards ahead. Only a little farther.

The footsteps were getting closer. They were running out of time. Rick ran ahead to get the shed open. He set

Shelly down to one side, where she would be out of sight, and searched for the fake rock that held the key to the padlock securing the double doors. He started kicking rocks over, frantically trying to find the right one. It was a matter of seconds now. Natalie finally caught up and stood with Shelly, trying to catch her breath. He could hear her practically gasping for air.

"What's wrong?" Her voice was breathy and low.

"I can't find the key. It's in one of those fake rocks." He kept looking. Natalie bent down and started scanning the rock bed surrounding the shed. Then she pointed.

"There. That one looks different than the others."

Rick looked where she was pointing. It took him a moment and then he saw it. He picked it up and sure enough, the key was tucked inside. He quickly put it in the lock and got the doors open. There was only one quad inside and the seat wasn't big enough for three. He would have to make it work. He quickly rolled it outside and started it up. At least it had some gas. How much, he had no idea.

"Get on." He helped Shelly up first, then Natalie. He squeezed himself in close to the handlebars, keeping Shelly sandwiched between them to shield her, as Natalie wanted. He hit the throttle just as a bullet hit the corner of the shed, sending a chunk of wood shooting past his face. That was too close.

The shots kept coming. He could hear each time the gun was fired over the roar of the quad's engine. He pulled down on the throttle, and they were propelled forward along the uneven ground. He had no idea how bad this was going to be for Natalie's injuries, assuming they didn't get shot. Branches from thick bushes scraped the legs of his jeans as they moved along the rough terrain. Natalie's arms wrapped around him from behind, pressing Shelly into his back. He was glad she did. They probably would have fallen off if she hadn't.

The path was narrowing. Two trees ahead looked a little too close together. He wasn't sure the quad would fit through. When another bullet hit a tree right next to them, sending bark splintering through the air, he pressed on. *Lord, please let us make it through this. Don't let his aim be true. Please help me protect the innocent.*

They just barely slipped through the trees, his jeans skimming the edges on both sides. Then the shots started coming in rapid succession, splitting off chunks of bark and small branches all around them. Too close to their heads. Natalie's arms pulled tighter. Shelly's head pressed deeper into his back. With every bullet that missed, Rick knew their odds of being shot were getting higher. Then he felt Natalie jolt forward. Was she hit?

THIRTEEN

It was difficult to breathe. Natalie's ribs ached as she pressed against Shelly's back. Her arms were becoming fatigued trying to hold on to Rick. The rough trail only exacerbated the pain in her ribs. That last bump shot through her like a bolt of lightning. With each reverberation of the gun, she half expected a bullet to hit her in the back. She just hoped that if it did, it would stop with her. That it wouldn't go all the way through her to Shelly. It was a strange moment to realize Shelly turned eight today and very likely didn't remember. If they survived the morning, she would find a way to do something to acknowledge the child's birthday.

When the next bullet came, she felt it whiz by the side of her head. Natalie's hair blew forward and as she turned, strands of hair broke away and disappeared into the forest like dust in the wind. That shot had been no more than a few centimeters from making real contact. If the trail had caused the quad to bump the wrong way in that moment, she would have been gone. Then she realized Rick's arm was bleeding. He was so much bigger than her that his arms and shoulders spread out above and outside her own body. She looked along the muscles of his arm, trying to determine if it was a scrape or if the bullet had penetrated. Whichever it was, it hadn't even made him flinch. This made her hopeful that it was only a scrape. *Please, Lord, don't let Rick or anyone else be injured trying to protect us. Please continue to stop the killer from hitting his mark. Help the police to catch him before he takes another victim.*

The quad bumped and jerked around a curve and then zoomed forward through a narrower opening in the trees and bushes. Thin branches and leaves brushed along her arms and the jeans covering her legs. She wondered if it was worse for Rick since his body was so much wider. It felt like a long time before the quad began to slow down. That was when she realized there hadn't been any more bullets since the one that sliced through her hair and along Rick's arm. That meant that they must have gotten enough distance between them and the shooter to finally be out of range. They needed to get to the police station. That seemed like the only logical way to find safety after what just happened.

There was a sputtering and then the motor turned off and they rolled to a stop. Rick was very still for a moment before he released his grip on the handles. "We're out of gas. But I think we're okay for now." He climbed off and then lifted Shelly off the seat and set her on the ground. Before Natalie could get up, he clasped her waist and carefully put her on her feet. He didn't say anything for a moment. He seemed to be concentrating on something. Then he looked down at her. "There's no way he could have kept up on foot. That doesn't mean he can't track us here. We need to get out of town. Whoever he is, he has some kind of access to what the police know. I don't see how else he keeps finding you."

Shelly leaned against Natalie. She put her arm around

her niece and rubbed her back. She considered what Rick was saying. He was right. She already suspected that the killer was a local. He could be friends with someone who knew where they were. "Should we go to the police station?"

Shaking his head, Rick said, "No. They'll just put us in another location. That guy will keep coming. We need to get out of the area so he doesn't know where to look. I have an army friend a few towns over that no one here knows about. We can lay low with him until this guy is locked up."

"If we can get out of town I would like to go home."

"We don't know how much information this guy has access to. We need to go somewhere that has no connection to either of us. My friend served with me. He has no link to this town."

Natalie considered what he was saying. It made sense. She didn't like it and there was no way to know how long they would be stuck in a stranger's house but what was the alternative? "Do you think he'll really take us in?"

"I know he will." His tone was so absolute it made Natalie wonder how he was so sure. What kind of bond had they formed when they were in the army? Was it one of the people he'd saved?

"Okay, then how do we get there? The bridge won't be fixed for at least a week." She looked around at the cover of trees. The birds were singing here. They were far enough from the fire and the shooter for things to almost seem normal. She could hear the rush of the river. It was close. Then she noticed blood dripping down Rick's arm. "Your arm. I saw the bullet go by my head. How bad did it get you?" She moved toward him, ready to help.

Rick looked down at his wound. It was a thin line

along the outside of his upper arm. He brushed away the blood and looked at her. "It's a scrape. Nothing to worry about." He glanced toward the direction of the water and then back at her. "We have to go out on a raft. I'm very comfortable navigating rough water. I've done it my whole life. I'll need to go into town to get what we need, though. I won't risk going back to my cabin. It would be too far from here to go on foot anyway."

Shaking her head, Natalie said, "It's too rough for her." She nodded toward her niece.

Shelly looked up. "We can do it. We have to get away from that man." Always so tenacious.

"Are you sure?" When Shelly nodded, Natalie turned to Rick. "You can really get us across with it being so rough? I can hear it from here. And Pete seemed to think it wasn't possible to do it safely."

"I've been on it when it was worse. Most people don't have my experience. And we're running out of places to hide. It's a risk but no worse than what we face here. I know I can get us across. I should have just done that to begin with." He didn't seem the least bit concerned. She supposed she should take comfort in that.

"Where do we get a raft? Do you know of another shed? Like where you got that quad?" She was beginning to realize she hadn't gotten to know this area at all. Now, she never intended to try. All she wanted was to leave this place.

"If there is one, I don't know about it. I have to go into town." He hesitated, which made Natalie wary of what he was about to say. "I need to hide you somewhere. I'll move faster on my own. I don't want to risk bringing the two of you out in the open again. This guy is too bold." When Natalie started shaking her head, knowing she had no defense against the masked man's strength, Rick continued, "I have a place that no one knows about. Even if he walked right by he wouldn't see you. You'll be safe there for the half an hour that I'll be gone." He stepped closer. "I would never do this if I believed there was any possibility that he could find you."

"Suppose you go into town and come back here unscathed and we're still here. What's to stop him from following you?"

He took a breath and looked down at Shelly, then at Natalie. "My training. I know how to make sure that doesn't happen. That's not to say that if he sees me carrying what we need that he won't try to find us. All we can do is hope we make it out before he does."

There wasn't really any choice. The police were getting picked off trying to protect them. If things kept going this way, there wouldn't be any left. That was unacceptable. She nodded her head.

"It isn't far from here." He turned and started walking.

Natalie took Shelly's hand and followed. It was no more than five minutes before he stopped again. It was hard to imagine how he knew his way around these woods. Everything looked the same. Trees of varying heights and bushes of all sizes.

"I'm hoping it's still here. I built it with my sister when we were kids. It was our secret place. No one else ever knew about it." He started pulling on some branches. Then he smiled. "C'mon. I'll hold it open. Go inside." He stood waiting.

Natalie reluctantly crouched down and looked through the opening. It was a little dark, making it difficult to see what was inside. She went in with Shelly close behind. Within a big cluster of dense bushes was a thick canvas structure held up by big branches that had been secured together by twine to create the framework of an open rectangular space. As she sat down in the corner on a pile of dead leaves, with Shelly settling next to her, Rick crawled in behind them. It wasn't high enough to stand up but they could move around on their knees.

"If you're uncomfortable staying in here I'll bring you with me. I just think—"

Natalie interrupted. "No. This makes sense. No one can see this from outside. I couldn't. We'll slow you down."

"I wish I didn't have to leave you here. But I can't think of another way to get us to the other side safely." He looked down at Shelly. "Want me to bring you a snack from the store?"

"Yes, please." She threw her arms around him. "You'll come back?"

He looked at Natalie as he put his arm around Shelly's back. "Nothing could keep me away." His expression was a mix of emotions that made him difficult to read. It almost seemed as if he was trying to stop himself from feeling anything.

He released Shelly and started crawling through the entrance of the bush fort. "I won't be long. Stay quiet. If anyone comes through here calling your names, don't respond. Even if they identify as police. It could be him trying to lure you out. If his skills are as good as I think they are, he'll track the quad. We're not far from there."

Natalie called, "Be careful."

A moment later, the green canvas was pressed back into place with the branches blocking the little bit of light that had been filtering in. They couldn't hear Rick walking away. She wasn't sure if it was the insulation of the leaves and branches wrapped around the canvas, or if he was just that quiet.

"Don't worry, Aunt Natty, he'll come back. He said he would." Shelly was trying to reassure her. Natalie didn't like that her niece was able to see that she was nervous. She was supposed to be making Shelly feel safe. Not making her feel as though she had to comfort her aunt. It was almost surprising how confident Shelly was in Rick. Natalie wasn't sure how much more he would want to endure to protect them. They were essentially strangers to him. He could just walk away and be done with all of this. But something in her gut told her Rick would be back. That Shelly's instincts about him were right.

She pulled Shelly to her side. "I know he will. Rick is a good man. How are you doing?" She hugged her niece in closer.

"I'm tired. I wish we could go home instead of to his friend's house."

"Me, too. I think Rick is right, though. We'll be safer in a new place, where no one knows us. Are you cold?" She rubbed her hand up and down Shelly's arm.

"A little, but I'm fine." She nuzzled in closer. "How long do you think we'll have to be on the raft?"

Shelly was shivering but felt warm. Her fever was coming back. That's when Natalie realized they left everything back at the motel. Including Shelly's medication. They had nothing. No clothes. No supplies. And nothing to keep Shelly's fever down or stop her ear infection from getting worse. They would have to deal with that when they got to Rick's friend's house. She wished she had remembered before he left. He could have picked up what Shelly needed while he was getting the raft. Then she realized she hadn't mentioned life jackets. How much could he carry on his own? What if he assumed Shelly could swim? It was probably best not to mention any of these concerns to her. No sense in getting her upset over things they couldn't control.

"I don't know. I wouldn't think it would be very long. I don't know how deep we are in the woods. I imagine we'll have to travel down the river a little before going to the other side. The edges are too rocky over there in the woodsy section. Do you remember?"

Shelly nodded. She seemed as though she was about to say something when the branches started moving outside. They scraped against the canvas doorway. It was too soon for Rick to be back. Light came through the crack between the fabric panels. They shouldn't have been talking. They should have kept their voices to a whisper. The bushes along the front of the fort were shifting the canvas. Someone was moving into the entrance.

They grabbed each other tighter, and Natalie held her breath as the canvas door began to shake with the movement of the branches. She absently began begging God for help. To stop whoever was about to come in. Shelly gasped as the bottom corner of the thick green fabric lifted. They both braced for whatever was about to happen. There was no other way in or out. The entire fort was enmeshed within dense branches that were at least two feet thick on all sides. Natalie was frozen in place as she waited to see the killer who had tracked them to this very spot.

FOURTEEN

Rick moved quickly through the forest. He purposely broke some little branches in the direction he was moving and pressed some leaves into the path along the way, hoping the killer would follow his trail if he was tracking them. When he came out of the trees at the end of Main Street, Rick finally slowed his pace. He took another look at the wound on his arm as he walked along the sidewalk. It was a little deeper than he'd thought. He hadn't even felt it happen. The thought of how close that bullet had come to hitting Natalie lit a wave of fury in him. He wanted to face off with the masked man without Natalie or Shelly around. If he didn't have to worry about their safety, he could be far more efficient in his attack.

When he first encountered the masked man behind his cabin, he'd stayed to protect Natalie and Shelly when the assailant ran off. That had been a mistake. If he'd gone after the man and stopped him, nothing that followed would have happened. If he would have thought to at least pull the mask off the killer's head in Natalie's cottage, there wouldn't have been a need for him to pursue them any further. His identity would have been known. He would have had to run. Rick shook his head trying to push away the what-if's. There was no point to dwelling on any of that. All he could do was make better choices going forward.

After a quick stop at the pharmacy for first-aid supplies for his arm, he went to Arnie's general store. The front windows were boarded up with plywood. He wondered if anyone had been hurt when the assailant shot out the windows. It was still hard to believe this was happening in Maple Rapids. Nothing exciting had ever happened when he was a kid. It had always been a peaceful place to visit. He still had to call his parents to tell them about the damage to the cabin. He knew they'd be upset, but not as relieved as they'd be to know he was safe. Maybe that was why he hadn't called them yet. Rick couldn't honestly tell them he was out of danger. Once he got Natalie and Shelly settled in his friend's house, he'd make that call. For now, it was better for his parents if they didn't know about any of it.

Inside the store, some of the shelves toward the front windows had been removed. The register was now at the back. Other than that, everyone was going about their business like they usually did. Dan came out from the back room and started helping some of the regular guys with hunting supplies while Rick looked for the raft and a few other things. When he walked up to the counter, he remembered telling Shelly he'd bring her something to eat.

"Dan, would you mind holding these aside while I run to the grocery section?"

"No problem, Rick. I'll keep it right here. When you're ready, I'll check you out." Dan was always friendly. He was one of the nicest people in town.

When Rick walked away, Dan went back to helping Jack McKenna and Tom Beckett. They'd been on the street watching when he and Natalie had brought Shelly to the doctor. They seemed to be eyeing Rick again now. He didn't like it. They both fit the physical appearance of the killer. Come to think of it, who was to say it wasn't both of them working together? Rick shook his head. He was getting paranoid. He couldn't start accusing every man in town of being a killer.

Once he found a few snacks he knew Natalie and Shelly liked, based on what they ate when Pete brought food, he started heading back over to Dan. That's when Henry Wilson walked in. The man had also taken interest in them outside the doctor's office. No one knew much about Henry. He was friendly enough most of the time but he sometimes had an odd way about him. Today was one of those times. He was covered in dirt, his camouflage pants and long sleeve T-shirt a mess. Rick took a closer look as their paths crossed. Henry's hands were dirty as well. Not his face, though. Except for around his eyes. That wasn't necessarily proof of guilt. Lots of guys covered their faces when they went hunting.

"Hey, Rick." Henry nodded his head. His eyes were sharply taking in everything around him. He gave Rick a quick once-over, as well, which wasn't really unusual for him.

"Hello, Henry. Where are you coming from?" Rick asked. Would he be able to tell if Henry was lying?

"I was out getting my dinner. I lost my best knife in the woods. I need a new one to get the meat processed and into the freezer. I should be set through the fall after today." He grinned a little. Henry didn't seem to be lying. But if he was the masked man, he would probably be comfortable with dishonesty.

As they walked toward the back, Rick tried to keep some distance from Henry. No chance of that since they were both headed to the same place—the knife case where Rick had left the rafting supplies, close to the register.

As they approached, Dan, Jack and Tom watched them.

"I've got everything right here for you, Rick." Dan stepped away from the other two men. They probably weren't there to buy anything today. Some of the guys liked to come in to see what was new and chat with each other, share hunting tales.

Henry seemed to take note of what Dan was referring to. "You going on a rafting trip?" He turned to Rick.

"Nah, just refreshing some old supplies. Making sure I have what I need when I do."

"Hmph. That's an awful lot. What'd a raccoon get into your stuff?" If this was any other day these questions would feel like benign chatter. Right now, it felt like something else entirely.

"Yeah." That was all Rick said. He wasn't great with lying. Best to keep his answers short. He put the bag from the pharmacy down on the counter along with the food he'd picked up on the other side of the store. Then he pulled out his wallet.

Just when Dan was about to start ringing things up, Arnie came out from the back room. He was moving a little slower than normal, his limp more pronounced. "Dan, why don't you take care of Henry? I can ring for Rick."

"Sure thing." He turned to Rick. "I'd wait to go rafting until the water settles down."

"I intend to. No one would be safe in those rapids today." Rick turned to Arnie as Dan walked to the other end of the counter to help Henry with the knife he wanted.

Arnie held a little extra weight under his loose clothes. Rick asked about the limp when he first came back into town, and Arnie had said it was an old injury that acted up when the rain came in.

"I guess this weather hasn't been doing you any favors." Rick was trying to blend in. To act like he would any other day. That meant making light conversation when all he really wanted to do was get back into the woods and get Natalie and Shelly out of the area.

"No, sir. It's been a rough couple days with the leg. And there's another storm brewing." Arnie scanned each item slowly, taking his time. Rick tried to hide his frustration.

"The sun is out. Did you see a weather report?"

Arnie chuckled a little and patted his leg. "Don't need to. I can feel it." He continued scanning. Once he was done, Rick paid and then started loading everything into the backpack he bought. He would have to carry the raft, which would definitely slow him down on the way back to the fort.

"You need help getting that out to your truck?" Arnie was always quick to offer a hand, either his own or one of his employees'.

"No thanks, I've got it." Rick started for the door.

"Have a nice day," Arnie called from behind the counter.

When Rick turned to give him a forced friendly smile, he noticed that Jack, Tom, Henry and Dan were all watching him go. Jack and Tom started walking toward him but Rick kept up his pace and went out the door. He moved quickly along the sidewalk. When he checked, Jack and Tom were watching him from the front of the store. Either they were up to no good or they thought Rick was. Whatever it was, he didn't like it. When he reached the opening in the trees he came through earlier, he glanced back to see if they were still staring. No one was outside. If they were keeping track of him, he had no idea where from.

When he was about halfway back, storm clouds started moving in, the sky darkening very quickly. Arnie's leg was right. Rick started moving faster, hoping to get across the river before the storm hit. A small rumble of thunder was followed by a quick flash of lightning in the distance. They still had a little time. But not much. Rick broke into a jog. He couldn't full-out run with all that he was carrying. And the wound on his arm was stinging. He still needed to patch that up, but with the storm coming in, he'd have to wait until they got to the other side of the river.

When he arrived at the fort, what he saw made him drop everything on the ground. *Lord, please don't let this be what it looks like.* Taking a quick turn in every direction, Rick looked for any signs of other people. He listened for movement. Nothing. He turned back to the bush fort and took a step forward. The branches were pulled away. Some had snapped off. The canvas door had been shoved aside. A small smear of fresh blood was streaked along the fabric. He crouched down and looked inside. Natalie and Shelly were gone. And there was blood. Not a lot, but any amount was a bad indication of what might have happened to them.

He should never have left them alone. He called their names but there was no response. He stood up and yelled out again. Nothing. What would he do now? How would he find them? He had no idea. And if he did manage to track them in the rain, would they even be alive by the time he got to them?

FIFTEEN

Raindrops made little tapping sounds on the leaves above. The static-charged air shifted as the wind began to kick up. Branches creaked and groaned. The animals had tucked themselves away, knowing before anyone else that the rain was coming. They always knew when something was about to happen. They could feel it in the atmosphere, their senses able to pick up the incremental signals nature gave them. If only people could feel those little warnings. Maybe then Natalie and Shelly would be safe.

Rick walked around the bushes that circled the canvas fort he'd made with his sister all those years ago. He tried to find footprints or some indication of what direction they'd been taken. With the rain falling, anything that had been there was gone. The anguish of what could be happening to them was tearing him apart. This was worse than what happened on the mission overseas. Back then, there hadn't been any reason to believe there was danger. This time, he knew there was a dangerous killer hunting them. He knew the risk and made the wrong call. This was truly on him. He was finally beginning to see the difference. There hadn't been any way for him to have anticipated what was going to happen on that mission. Maybe it was finally time to let that go. To forgive himself for not being able to save everyone. To be grateful that he had survived. That he might one day find love. That he could build a life. First he needed to find Natalie and Shelly before it was too late.

He told himself not to imagine the worst. They had to be out there. But doubt and fear twisted his gut into a painful knot.

Looking up into the gray sky, with drops of rain falling into his eyes, he threw himself on God's mercy. "Show me the way." It came out as a whisper at first. "They don't deserve this." Louder, he called up toward the clouds, "Please! Point me in the right direction!" He dropped to his knees in the muddy leaves. "I'm begging You, Lord, help me save them. I need to save them." His body fell forward, his hands sinking into the wet ground. Then he looked up again, his voice cracking. "If not for me, for them."

The snap of a branch brought his head around. The last thing he needed to deal with right now was some bear looking for food. He got on his feet and scanned the area. There was no movement. No sound. Then another crunch. This time he pinpointed the direction. He considered that the masked man was coming back for him. Rick hoped he would. He'd drag him down Main Street to the police station if he had to.

Footsteps. Someone was definitely coming. Silently, he made his way behind a thick tree trunk. His ears perked up, tracking the sounds. Whispering. Was that what he was hearing? He leaned his head out and relief flooded his veins.

"You're alright? What happened?" he asked as he ran forward. Rick couldn't believe his eyes. He silently thanked God. Natalie and Shelly were right there in front of him. Alive and seemingly well.

Natalie smiled at him. Nothing bad could have happened if she was smiling, could it? He waited. Watched her and Shelly as they looked at each other, then back at him.

"We were in the fort talking when we heard noise. The branches started moving and the door flap began to lift. We thought he found us." She shook her head with disbelief in her eyes. Rick was very anxious for her to tell him who it was. "But then a raccoon came in. He looked just as surprised to see us as we were to see him. He let out this wild sound and tried to run. He got caught up in some branches before he got away. We decided to get out of there in case he came back."

"There was blood. Did he bite one of you?"

She shook her head. "I think he may have gotten cut. He got a little frazzled trying to get away from us."

"Where did you go? I called out your names."

"We went looking for a place to hide. We found a good spot and waited. I thought I heard you yelling so we came back." Something shifted in her expression. "We lost Shelly's medication in the fire. Her fever is coming back. We'll need to get her to a doctor to get antibiotics when we get where we're going."

Rick ran over to his backpack and started digging for the bag from the pharmacy. "When I went into town I grabbed some stuff for the cut on my arm and remembered Shelly lost her meds. I don't have the antibiotics but I did get the liquid Advil." He handed the box to Natalie.

"Thank you, Rick. I never would have thought you'd think of that." She quickly pulled out the bottle and poured the purple liquid. Shelly drank it down without protest.

She had that red watery look in her eyes again. He'd make sure she got to a doctor at some point.

"We need to get moving. We've been out here too long. The river will only get—" He stopped himself. He didn't want to scare Shelly. "I have PFDs for both of you. You can put them on down by the water while I inflate the raft." He swung the backpack over his shoulder and grabbed the rest of what he'd dropped on the ground.

"Do you need help?" Natalie's dark curls were hanging down along her face from the rain.

"You take Shelly. I've got this stuff." He started walking when Natalie lifted Shelly into her arms. She seemed to be moving a little better. It wasn't far to the river's edge.

He gave Natalie the personal flotation devices and then got the pump going on the raft. It was a small one. It was going to be a tight fit. He'd chosen it so it wouldn't be too heavy to lug through the woods. But he was questioning that decision. He wasn't sure it would stay afloat with all of them in it, now that he saw how rough the water was. The river was shifting in all directions, bursts of water whipping around and spraying the air. But there was no time to debate his plan. There was no other option. They had to go.

"I want the two of you to get in and hold the paddles for me. I'm going to push the raft in and jump on. Then I'll need you to follow my instructions to help me guide the raft. Can you do that?" He was looking at Natalie. Drops of water streamed down her soft skin. When she nodded, he helped each of them into the raft and handed her the paddles. Once he had it pushed halfway in, he stepped in and pushed off with his other foot.

He took one of the paddles and sat in the front. "Put yours out to the left. Turn it flat." He put his out to the right and began to steer. The rapids threw them up and down. The raft shifted to the side, nearly tipping. He leaned his body to right it. He called out instructions while he did his part to keep them from flipping.

When Natalie let out a small squeal, he turned back to check on them and saw Shelly burrowed in Natalie's arms. The paddle was gone.

"The current pulled the paddle right out of my hands. Shelly nearly fell in." Her tone was full of anguish. Shelly didn't look much better. He couldn't do anything to comfort them. He had to focus or they wouldn't make it.

Fighting the current and the sudden lifts and drops, Rick guided them along. He could see the damaged bridge in the distance. Thunder rumbled and echoed all around them. A streak of lightning shot across the sky and dipped down, splitting a large tree on the bank just ahead of them. The smaller section snapped off and fell into the river. Right in their path. Rick frantically worked to shift the direction of the raft. Then he heard the reverberation of a rifle. He turned to look for the shooter. To see if it was the killer or some diehard hunter out in this weather. With his movement, the boat twisted and began to lift sideways. Shelly let out a muffled scream and he could hear Natalie trying to calm her. He pressed all of his weight against the elevated side of the raft, praying they wouldn't be tossed into the angry river. As the raft leveled, he thought they were safe until another gunshot rang out.

"Get down!" He reached over and pressed on Natalie's shoulder. "He's out there. Stay low."

Natalie quickly covered her niece with her own body. When the next shot burst into the air, Rick was able to find the source. The killer was standing on the shoreline, the ski mask covering his face, and he was taking aim.

Rick put his body over Natalie's, but as water began to flood into the raft, he sat up and saw the hole in the now deflating boat.

"We have to swim for it. I'll take Shelly. You grab on to me. Let's try to get to the other side. Once we're inside the trees, he won't be able to get to us." There was no time to debate it or to go into detail. Rick pulled Shelly into his arms and let himself slide into the water. Natalie followed. He held Shelly's head above water and turned his body sideways to shield her from the shooter. The shots kept coming. He saw some of them slice through the water not far from where he swam.

Using all his strength, he made for the other side, but the current was pulling him back to the wrong shore. He felt Natalie's grip on the waistband of his jeans tugging from the way the current was dragging her. His legs kicked with everything he had but the water was too strong. He glanced back and saw the gunman moving quickly along the shoreline. At least they were moving faster than he could run, making it difficult for him to be able to aim with any accuracy. Their bodies bobbed up and down and spun in every direction as the river dragged them toward the damaged bridge. He tried to grab on to the frame as they passed under, but he was yanked away. He glanced back to check on Natalie. The life preserver was keeping her head above water. A sudden shift in the current nearly pulled them under, then whirled them up and onto the shore a small distance from the bridge. They crawled in the dirt and collapsed.

Through labored breaths, Rick tried to speak. "We can't stay here. He's coming." He kept panting, trying to steady himself. "Have to move. Now." There was no chance they would get very far. Tears rolled from Shelly's eyes as she gasped for air and Natalie could barely catch her breath. Rick dragged himself up and then pulled each of them to their feet.

"We need a minute. We can't run like this." Natalie's words were broken up by her attempts to steady her breathing.

"I get it. We just need to get out of sight." He lifted Shelly into his arms and started walking. He wasn't in any condition to run, either. "We'll find a place to hide." He wasn't even sure she heard him. As long as he could hear her walking behind him, he would keep going. He saw a patch of tall bushes that reminded him of where he and his sister built their fort. He knew there was a good chance it could be fairly hollow inside, where the sun didn't reach. He set Shelly on the ground and got on his hands and knees.

Once he got a good look, he waved them toward him. "We'll wait it out in here." He pulled the branches back so they could crawl through. Natalie urged Shelly in first. Then she went in. Rick hurried in behind her when he heard someone running in their direction. He tried to steady the bush but he had no idea if he was fast enough. He put his finger to his lips to quiet Shelly's whimpering.

Twigs broke under the weight of someone's feet. Then there were legs no more than two feet from where they were crouched inside the bushes. The rifle stock swung down and rested on the ground like a cane. It was definitely him. He'd found their tracks in the mud by the water. Rick had to hope they hadn't left a trail into the bushes. But this was one time the rain may have been to their advantage. By the way the gunman's legs twisted, turning in every direction, he hadn't seen any footprints and was trying to figure out which way they might have gone. He stood there for what felt like an eternity. If he looked into the bushes, he'd have an easy target. There was no way for them to get out fast enough. No way for Rick to get ahold of the rifle before the killer could pick them off. He chastised himself for not positioning himself differently so he would have been able to strike. Not that he had the energy to fight yet.

They all stayed silent, waiting to see what the gunman would do. To their horror, he lifted the rifle and turned toward the bush. Could he see them? Was he about to take his shot?

SIXTEEN

The rain-soaked ground was sinking beneath Natalie's feet. She wasn't sure how much longer she could remain still in this awkward crouched position. Her knees and back were beginning to ache. Keeping herself from shivering felt nearly impossible. They were all soaked and drained from the exertion of swimming through that wild current and then having to keep moving after finally washing ashore. Shelly was pressed against her side, needing the support to stay still. Rick's expression was so intense. Every muscle in his body was rigid, as if he was ready to spring into action at any moment.

When those legs finally moved away, they all released the air they had been holding. Rick put his hand up, signaling for them to remain still. He held it there until they could no longer hear footsteps. The only sounds came from the roar of thunder and the rain beating down on the bushes surrounding them.

"Can we move now?" Shelly's plea was a reminder that she was still sick. Her voice held the fatigue she clearly felt. Her eyes were watery and red. Being wet and cold was only going to make her get worse. Especially without access to the medication she needed.

"Of course. Let's get out of here." Rick pushed aside

the branches and held them for her to crawl out. Natalie followed. Rick stepped out and immediately scanned their surroundings.

"How far do you think we are from the police station?" Natalie just wanted to get Shelly somewhere safe so she could rest. If that meant sleeping on the couch in Pete's office, then that's what they'd do.

"I have something else in mind. It's in the opposite direction of where the gunman was going when he walked away and I'd like to regroup without anyone knowing where we are."

Natalie was about to protest, then stopped herself. Rick had been right about going into town in the police car drawing too much attention. And he was right that the river was their best way out. If the gunman hadn't shown up, they'd be on their way out of this place right now. And he'd done well at traversing the rough rapids until a bullet punctured the raft. She'd give his plan a chance this time. The one thing she was sure of was that he had their best interests at heart. She also believed that God had brought her to his door for a reason. He had the experience that she didn't when it came to navigating a hostile environment. When she nodded her acceptance, relief was written all over his face.

"Hey, how about if I give you a piggyback ride?" He smiled down at Shelly, who was more than happy to climb right on.

"Did you know? I'm eight today." Shelly said it as if everything was perfectly normal. Natalie was stunned that she remembered.

"Eight, huh? That's pretty old." He started walking. "I guess we'll have to do something to celebrate."

"Okay." Shelly rested her head on his shoulder. Natalie rubbed her back and smiled at her, trying to be reassuring.

She wanted to ask how far they had to go. She wasn't sure how much more she could endure in this weather. As if in answer to her thoughts, Rick spoke up.

"It's maybe ten minutes from here. A lot closer than getting back to the middle of town. If you need to take a break, just let me know. We'll stop." He looked at her with concern. He knew she was still injured.

They trekked through the mud-slicked path a little slower than they probably should have. When they arrived at the back door of a B and B on the outskirts of town, Rick led Natalie inside. They entered into a well-equipped kitchen with fresh rolls cooling on the stone countertop. Rick set Shelly down in a chair. He grabbed a few rolls and handed one to each of them. Natalie couldn't help but worry how the owner would react seeing them there with mud and water tracked across the white tile floor. Never mind taking food without permission.

"The owner is an old friend. She won't mind if we eat something. We'll wait here until she comes in so no one sees us." He pulled open the industrial-size refrigerator door, took bottles of water and gave one to Natalie. He opened Shelly's before handing it to her.

With a little reluctance, Natalie took a bite of the roll. It felt a little strange but Rick said the owner was a friend. If someone she cared about came to her in this situation, she wouldn't mind if they ate her food. The roll was dense and soft. The warmth was exactly what she needed. She wasn't sure if it was the best roll she'd ever had, or if she was just so hungry that anything would taste good in that moment. Rick and Shelly ate theirs just as quickly.

Rick was reaching for another roll when a woman came

through the swinging door. She stopped short, startled by their presence. She was slim, like a runner, with dirty blond hair and big blue eyes. She wore cropped tan pants and a sleeveless white button-down with brown loafers. When her eyes landed on Rick, recognition sparked.

"Rick? What happened? What are you doing in here?" She came toward him, worry tensing her features. They shared a quick embrace. She stared up at him with genuine concern in her eyes.

"It's a long story. I need somewhere to lay low for the night. I don't want anyone to know where we are."

She glanced at Natalie and Shelly and then back toward him. "Wait here. I'll make sure there's a clear path and get you up to a room. I only have one open right now, on the top floor. Will that work? There are two double beds."

"Yes. Thank you." A look passed between them and then she started back toward the door. She hesitated and turned back to them.

She spoke in a quiet voice. "Take anything you want to eat or drink." Then she went back through the swinging door.

Natalie had never known people who would help this way with no questions asked, outside of her family. This was a testament to the kind of man Rick was. From what she'd seen, everyone he knew not only seemed to respect him, but they were also willing to extend themselves to help him.

Rick took a container of sliced turkey from the fridge and set it on the table. Natalie pressed her hand to Shelly's forehead and then the back of her neck. At least her fever was coming down. She sat next to her niece and made sandwiches on the warm rolls. They really were as good as she thought when she'd eaten the first one.

"I've known Ashley since we were kids. Her family has had this place for a few generations. We can trust her," Rick said between bites of the sandwich.

"Shelly needs another bottle of antibiotics. Does the pharmacy in town deliver?"

Rick seemed to mull it over. "They used to. It certainly wouldn't hurt to ask. I'd prefer not to risk going back there if we can avoid it for now." He pulled a small baggie out of his pocket. It looked similar to a sandwich bag with the slider along the top, but it was much thicker with an opaque texture. A waterproof bag, she realized when he pulled out his phone and called the pharmacy. He explained that the medication had been lost and asked if they could call the doctor to fill it again. He was able to get the pharmacist to agree to drop it off on his way home that evening and to keep it to himself. The pharmacist was an old friend of his parents. He'd delivered to them at the cabin when they used to come in the summers.

Soon after Rick was finished with his phone call, Ashley appeared and led them through a dining room and up a set of stairs to the top floor. Ashley explained that there were no other rooms on that level except the owner's suite, so no one would know they were in the B and B.

Once they were inside the room, Ashley closed the door and gestured toward a pile of clothes on the dresser.

"I grabbed some of my clothes for you to wear." She was addressing Natalie. "I think we're close enough in size. I also found a few things my nephew left here. It might be a little big on her but at least she'll be dry." She nodded toward Shelly. Then she turned to Rick. "You got some lost and found items that have been here long enough for me to be confident that no one is coming back to claim them." She looked back to Natalie. "I'm Ashley, by the way."

Rick stepped in to make the introductions. "I'm sorry. This is Natalie and her niece, Shelly. Thank you for doing this. You have no idea what we've been through in the last couple days. I'll settle up with you for the room and food once this is over."

"You'll do no such thing. We're friends. We help each other. I don't want to hear anything more about it."

"I appreciate that."

She nodded. "Now, I do have some idea what you're dealing with. I'm guessing these two are the ones you've been protecting from whoever is going around shooting people?"

"No secrets in this town." Rick smiled a little.

"There is now. I won't tell anyone you're here. Maybe Pete will be able to get this guy if he doesn't have to worry about having officers watching you. I have to get back downstairs. There're fresh towels in the bathroom. I'll bring more food up when I serve dinner." She turned to Rick. "If you guys need anything, call my cell. I'll bring it up. Don't risk popping out." Then she left the room.

Rick seemed to remember something. His eyebrows pressed together. He pulled out his phone. "I'll send her a text about the pharmacist coming later. That way she can bring the medicine up when it gets here." He tapped away on the screen and then put it on the dresser. "Do you want to take Shelly in to change?"

"I think I'm going to give her a quick shower." She took clothes for both her and Shelly and went into the bathroom. A hot shower was exactly what they all needed.

Once they were clean and wearing the borrowed clothes, the afternoon went by quietly in the comfortable room. Shelly slept on and off. Natalie relaxed enough to enjoy the stunning mountain view out the big window. When Ashley brought dinner, she included a cupcake for Shelly. Rick had sent her a text asking for something special for her birthday. The medication arrived soon after that. It wasn't long before they were tucking Shelly in for the night. They were all feeling more at ease now that no one knew where to find them. It meant that no one could accidentally mention their location in front of the man trying to kill them.

While Shelly slept, Natalie and Rick sat in the two wingback chairs talking quietly and playing cards. They shared things about their childhoods and their jobs. It felt so natural. Like spending time with an old friend. But it was also more. When their eyes met and held, Natalie felt a spark she'd never experienced before. Not even with Eric. It made her face heat a little. Thick lashes lined his stunning green eyes that held flecks of gold and blue. Wisps of light hair fell over his forehead. It was difficult to look away from his handsome face. She felt her heart beating faster and she wasn't sure what it meant or whether Rick was experiencing it, too. She got her answer when Rick leaned a little closer.

The ring of his phone had them both turning away. He glanced at the screen and then put it back on the table. This wasn't the first time he'd ignored a call.

"It's my brother-in-law. I can call him back."

"No, you should answer. Your family might be worried. We have no idea what might be on the news about what has been happening here." Natalie didn't want his family to worry about him.

"I guess you're right." He tapped the screen and put the phone to his ear. "Hey, Ben." He listened for a few moments and his face lit up. He looked so happy. A broad smile stretched wide. "You're sure? What else?" He stood up and listened. "That's great. Send me the info. I'll call tomorrow." He thanked his brother-in-law and ended the call.

"Good news?" Natalie couldn't help but be happy to see him this way. His excitement was contagious.

He was pacing the room. "You could say that. The offer came in. When they couldn't reach me, they called Ben." Realizing she had no idea what he was referring to, he continued. "That job in California. They want me to start in a few weeks. And the package is even better than I'd hoped."

"That's great. Congratulations. I'm really happy for you." Trying to hide the disappointment settling in the pit of her stomach, Natalie smiled and injected a little pep in her tone. How could she not be happy for him? He deserved to get what he wanted.

"I didn't think they'd make the offer. I definitely didn't expect it to be so good." He took his seat across from her. "Maybe you and Shelly could come visit sometime. There's so much to do there. We could take her to the amusement parks and the beach." His excitement was palpable.

"Maybe. That might be nice." She didn't know when they'd be able to get out there. Assuming they survived what was happening, Shelly would be starting school soon. Natalie would be teaching again, if her job was still there. She stretched her arms over her head and yawned. "I'm getting pretty tired. We should turn in." She stood up. "I'm really happy for you, Rick. You deserve this."

"Thanks."

Crawling into bed with Shelly, she turned away from

him. She couldn't let him see how disappointed she really was. After a few minutes, she heard him pull the covers back in the other bed and sit down, then the light went out. Natalie stared into the darkness for a long time. There were still so many unknowns. So much uncertainty about their survival. She closed her eyes and tried to pray. It was difficult to focus on anything but the fact that Rick would be moving to the other side of the country when this was over. It shouldn't bother her. It was what he wanted. And they really didn't know each other very well. Even if it was beginning to feel like they did. Maybe once she was back at home she would see it differently. She closed her eyes, hoping sleep would come.

It wasn't long before a sudden pounding on the door had them both sitting up. Ashley wouldn't intentionally do anything to bring attention to them. Something had to be wrong.

SEVENTEEN

When the sun eased in through the window, Rick opened his eyes. He didn't move. No sense in waking Natalie and Shelly. He was considering trying to get out on the river again. With the storm finally over, maybe the water wasn't as rough. Not that Pete Dennis would go along with it. Apparently, the pharmacist ran into Officer Hazel Clarke at the diner last night and let it slip that he'd brought Shelly's medication to the B and B. She came with Pete immediately after. Neither of them were pleased, as evidenced by their rapping on the guest-room door in the middle of the night.

Pete gave them a stern lecture about keeping their location hidden and he insisted on having an officer posted outside their door. He was only trying to do what he thought was right but Rick knew having the police around only put a bull's-eye on their location. At least the officer wasn't outside, where the killer could shoot him from a distance. Pete also told them that Officer Lee Kramer was alright. He'd been shot and fell off the motel porch before the fire was set. At least he would be okay. But they couldn't stay at the B and B now. It wasn't fair to Ashley or the other guests to put them in that kind of danger. Rick had to come up with another place for them to hide. He knew Pete was planning on taking them to an empty cabin with two officers to keep watch after breakfast. Hazel was probably stocking it with food right now.

Rick couldn't get the killer out of his mind. Now that the police were here, *he* probably knew where they were. *He.* Who was *he*? Could it really be someone Rick had known most of his life? He couldn't imagine anyone here doing what that masked man had done in the last few days. Pete told him they still hadn't found any sign of the woman Shelly saw him shoving into the river that night. There wasn't a single man living in town that Rick would believe capable of doing that. And he was usually very good at picking up on darkness in others. Even Pete was having a difficult time with that possibility. There were a few men who had been home alone when the attacks took place, including Jack McKenna, Tom Beckett, Henry Winston and Dan Caraway, but there was no evidence of their involvement. Maybe they each had exhibited some odd behavior in the days that followed, but was it really any different from how they had always been? Could it really be one of them?

With his head spinning in circles, he glanced at the time. He knew he had to call about the job offer but it was definitely too early to call California. It would only be four in the morning there. The job was exactly what he'd wanted, so why was he suddenly having doubts about accepting the position?

He glanced over at Natalie. She looked so peaceful as she lay there sleeping. He'd wanted to kiss her last night before the call came in from Ben. Would it be worth giving up this opportunity to see if there was something real between them? What if it was just the heat of the situation? Then he'd regret passing on the job. If he took it, would he regret missing out on what he could have with Natalie more?

His thoughts were interrupted when Natalie began whimpering in her sleep. She was gripping the blankets, her face strained. She seemed to be having another nightmare. He got up and gently rubbed her arm.

"Wake up. I think you're having a bad dream. Natalie?" He clasped her shoulder and gave a little nudge.

With a quick inhale, Natalie jolted upright in bed. She was a little breathless as she seemed to take in her surroundings. When she realized Rick was next to her, she shifted away and got out of bed.

"Are you okay?" Rick watched her walk over to the window.

"I just had a bad dream. I'm fine." Natalie moved back a few steps but she didn't turn to face him.

"The fire?"

She shook her head. "Not this time." When she didn't elaborate, he wasn't sure if he should ask. She seemed distant this morning. Had he imagined the connection between them? The light was dim in the room last night. They were both tired. Maybe it was one-sided. A faint knock on the door got her to turn from the window.

"It's Hazel." Her voice was low. "I'm here to escort you to the cabin when you're ready. Ashely told me she's bringing breakfast in a few minutes. We'll leave after that."

Natalie went over to Shelly and woke her up. They slipped quietly into the bathroom to wash up and put on fresh clothes. Rick did a quick change while they were in there. He'd brush his teeth when they came out. He thought more about the job. Maybe he was letting the intensity of everything that happened cloud his judgment.

He had been hoping for this offer for weeks. Why would he have doubts now?

Another knock at the door had Natalie back out in the room with Shelly. Ashley brought in a rolling table of food. When she left, they sat on the chairs and Rick took the edge of his bed. Everyone was quiet at first as they ate. Shelly dug into her food. She looked a little better. The sleep had done her some good, along with the medication.

Finally, Natalie broke the silence. "Is there any other way out of here? I was thinking, I have a distant cousin down south. I could probably go stay with him for a while. I doubt anyone would connect me to him. We haven't seen each other since we were kids. We only keep in touch on the holidays." Natalie leaned back in her chair. "He's former military, like you. I know you'll need to be heading west soon. I don't want you to feel obligated to stay with us."

Shelly looked up at him when Natalie said that last part. "Where are you going, Rick? You're not staying with us?"

"Of course I am." He turned to Natalie. "I intend on seeing this through."

"I know, but we have no idea who this guy is or when the police will catch him. If they ever do. I'm just being realistic. You can't pause your life indefinitely for us." She went back to eating.

What changed? Had he really imagined that she might be developing feelings for him? Maybe a fresh start in California wasn't such a bad idea after all.

Rick didn't bother to respond. He wasn't sure what to say. Did she want him to go? He let his mind drift while they ate breakfast. He thought about Maple Rapids and the people who lived here. The way a simple ride through town in a police car had brought so much unwanted attention. Then he realized what they should do. He jumped up and opened the door. Hazel was there with the officer, who had sat in the hallway most of the night. She stood up immediately, probably thinking something might be wrong.

"Is Pete coming before we go?" Rick needed to talk to him.

"I believe so. Why? Did something happen?" Hazel looked past him into the room.

"No, everything is fine in there. I need to run an idea by him. When will he be here?"

She glanced at her watch. "Any minute now."

"Good. I'll want you in on this, too."

"In on what?"

He gave her a brief summary of his idea. She explained why it wouldn't work. Then something else came to mind that would be risky in a different way, but had the potential to help them finally catch this guy. Hazel was reluctant at first, but once she understood what he had in mind, her eyes lit up and she agreed to talk to Pete about it once he arrived. There were parts of the plan that made Rick uneasy, but if it worked, this whole thing could be over by the end of the night. However, if it went wrong, he wasn't sure how he'd live with it.

Waiting in the room for Pete to arrive, Rick told Natalie his idea when Shelly went into the bathroom. She was quiet for a moment before she reacted.

"It could work. It'll be dangerous for you, though. I'm not sure how I feel about that. Why don't we try getting across the river again? Maybe Ashley has a raft here we can use. That way no one would see us buying it and the killer wouldn't find out."

"I mentioned that to Hazel. That was the plan I had initially when I went out there to talk to her. But it wouldn't be safe. No more rain is coming but the river's really churning with the wind kicking up. The police have already discussed this option and feel they couldn't cover us once we're in the water. And more police could be shot. This guy is a professional-level marksman. Lee was hit from a pretty good distance when he got up to stretch his legs. That's why we didn't hear anything. A silencer used at that distance would make it impossible to hear from inside the room. And since he dropped in the gravel instead of on the porch... Well, you get the idea." He saw the concern in her eyes. "And yes, he's going to be fine."

Natalie didn't look convinced. "Are you sure?"

"Pete or Hazel would've told me if he wasn't."

"You really think they would?"

"I do. I've known these people most of my life. They'd tell me if a friend took a bad turn."

She ran her fingers through the top of her hair and walked over to the window. "I don't want anyone else to get hurt over this." She stood quiet for a moment. "Do you really think this would work?" She turned to face him. "Without anyone else getting hurt?"

He knew he could never be sure of what would happen. "I can't guarantee the outcome but I think it's the best shot. You even said yourself that no amount of planning—"

She waved her hand as the door opened and Shelly came out. "Is it time to go?"

"Not yet. Why don't you go brush your hair. I think I saw a comb in the drawer where we found the toothbrushes." Natalie forced a smile. Rick had seen her do this before to keep Shelly calm. When her niece went back in, she pulled the door closed and gestured for Rick to follow her to the other side of the room.

He put his hand on her shoulder and leaned in close. "Neither one of us wants anything to happen to her. Everything else the police have tried has nearly gotten us all killed." He kept his voice low. "There aren't many places left to hide. The best thing we can do is draw him out on our terms and take him down."

"I don't like it but I can't think of anything better. What about the mask they pulled off the gunman in the woods near my cottage? Did they test that?"

"They didn't get anything usable from the mask."

With an exasperated breath, Natalie walked over and sat in one of the wingback chairs as Shelly came out, putting an end to the discussion. A knowing look passed between them. It was decided.

It wasn't long before Pete arrived and they were heading downstairs to leave. There were three police cars lined up and six officers waiting outside. Rick walked out first. Then Pete followed with his arm around the woman hidden under the blanket. Part of the plan was to keep her concealed. To let those who saw them wonder why and get them talking. They quickly slipped into the back seat of the middle car. The officers got in the front seats of all three cars and started driving. Rick looked back at Pete standing in front of the B and B. He nodded at Rick before they turned onto the road.

Three police cars driving together down Main Street drew a lot of attention, as Rick knew they would. He made sure to look out the window so people would see him. With a clear view of what could easily be assumed to be two people under a blanket, everyone would guess it was Natalie and Shelly. The idea that they were hiding that way would have people talking about it even more. This was what he wanted. If the masked man didn't see them, he would definitely hear about it before the day was out. People in town knew Pete's family had a hunting cabin. Given the direction the police cars turned to head up the mountain, everyone would speculate about the likelihood of where they were going.

Once they arrived at Pete's cabin, most of the officers left. Only two remained with one black-and-white car parked out front. The others went back into town with the intention of being seen. Then it was a matter of waiting until nightfall.

The hours went by slowly. Rick checked in with Pete just about every hour. He was beginning to question his plan by the time the sun went down but it was too late to change course. They had waited all day.

He stayed out in the main living area of the cabin with the intention of staying awake until this was over. The layout was basically the same as his family's cabin, but nothing had been updated in this one. When he checked his watch and realized it was after midnight, he really began to doubt his plan would work. Maybe the masked man figured out that it was a trap. Through the window, he checked on the officer on the porch. He looked alert, his head moving back and forth, seeming to be scanning the area. The idea of another officer getting hurt twisted in Rick's gut. There was a real possibility that it could happen again before this was over.

The hours kept ticking by. He finally sat down on the couch a little after four in the morning. The plan failed. Either the masked man hadn't heard about them parading through town, or he saw it for what it was. Rick eased back and gave in to his exhaustion. He slowly slid down until he was lying across the cushions, one foot still planted on the floor. He would just close his eyes for a few minutes.

He figured no one was coming, anyway. He didn't intend on falling asleep but his entire body was so fatigued. He could feel himself drifting in and out. The delirium had been taking hold for a few hours. He hoped Natalie and Shelly were able to sleep. He didn't want to risk waking them up by checking on them.

A familiar *tick, tick* followed by a thump quickly fired up Rick's senses. He lifted his head, his eyes just above the back of the couch. When the door started easing open, the cool night air invaded the warmth of the small space. Rick slid quietly off the couch and kneeled on the floor. He peeked around the side just in time to see the masked man walking in the direction of the bedroom. Rick bounded toward him before he could react, slamming him against the open door. They fought for the gun in his hand but he held it tight. They tumbled out the door, onto the porch.

Rick couldn't deny this man was not only strong, but also knew how to handle himself. They ended up crashing down the stairs into the dirt. Rick saw the officer bleeding a few feet away from them. It fueled his anger. He got in a few solid shots and was about to reach for the gun when Hazel called out.

"Drop the gun and get on your belly!" Her booming voice distracted them both, bringing Rick's attention to where she stood pointing her Glock toward the gunman.

The assailant quickly shifted behind Rick and held his gun to Rick's head. Hazel was taking aim, but Rick knew she couldn't make that shot safely in this darkness. The sky was cluttered with clouds, diminishing the moonlight and blocking the stars from view. He could see her squinting through the sight of her weapon. Then the gun next to his head went off. It wasn't anywhere near as loud as it could be, the silencer dampening most of the sound. Rick tensed with expectation, but it was Hazel who fell back through the door, out of sight. In the next moment, the butt of the gun came down on Rick's head. He was too disoriented to fight back. He'd never felt this helpless before. When the next blow came, Rick's last thoughts were of Natalie and Shelly.

He'd failed them.

EIGHTEEN

Natalie woke with a start. She'd barely slept. It would be dawn soon. She was looking forward to the morning sun to brighten the room. It had been an exceptionally dark night. Shelly stirred next to her and sat up.

"Can we get something to eat? I'm starving." Since getting sick, Shelly hadn't eaten nearly as much as she normally did. The fact that her appetite was coming back gave Natalie hope that she was getting better.

"I'm not sure. It's still pretty early." She took a quick look at the digital clock on the end table. "It's barely five. How hungry are you?"

She grabbed her tummy. "Really hungry."

Natalie got up and opened the door. Pete was sitting in a chair in the hall. He looked up at her. He had to be exhausted. He hadn't left his post since Rick left yesterday. Natalie had checked in with him several times.

"Have you heard anything?" The same question she asked every time she opened the door. She couldn't help but worry for Rick and the other officers.

"Hazel checked in about an hour ago. Nothing yet. She'll be checking in again soon. What are you doing up? You should try to sleep."

"Shelly is starting to feel better. She's hungry. Do you

think Ashley would mind if we went down to the kitchen and grabbed a little something?" It had been difficult to stay behind at the B and B and let Officer Hazel Clarke take her place. Rick made it sound so simple. Hazel pretends to be Natalie and Shelly by hiding under the blanket and carrying a duffel full of towels. She would keep the blanket on as they drove through town and then pretend to be asleep in the bedroom with her gun ready for when the killer came for them. Rick would be there as backup. Natalie knew he'd put himself in the line of fire before he let something happen to anyone else. The worry had kept her up most of the night. She lost count of how many times she'd prayed for Rick, Hazel and the other officer to be kept safe.

Pete stood up. "Ashley went downstairs a few minutes ago to start prepping for breakfast. I'll walk you down. I'm sure you're anxious to get out of the room. No one else is up. I haven't heard a sound. Would you like to eat in the dining room?"

"I would love that. The walls are starting to close in. I'll get Shelly." Her niece was already putting on the sneakers Ashley had given her when they'd arrived.

Down in the kitchen, Ashley was slicing fruit and baking fresh buns. The smell made Natalie's mouth water. Ashley looked up and smiled when they came through the swinging door. She had the nicest bed-and-breakfast Natalie had ever seen. It didn't have a lot of floral wallpaper or knickknacks on every flat surface. The decor felt fresh and airy. Neutral colors and subtle grass cloth wallpaper lined the walls, and tasteful vases with fresh flowers were on some of the tables. The paintings depicted local landscapes. It was warm and homey. Which only made her miss her own home even more.

"Good morning. I have cinnamon buns coming out in a few minutes. Would you like some?" Ashley wiped her hands on a towel. "I can make eggs, French toast, pancakes, maybe waffles? What are you craving this morning?"

Shelly spoke up before Natalie had the chance. "I think one of each."

"Coming right up." She focused on Pete. "Do you want me to bring it up or can they eat in the dining room?"

"I think we can stay down here for a little while. They're getting a little stir-crazy up there. We'll go back to the room before any guests come down. What time does that usually start happening?"

She glanced at a clock on the wall. "I think we have another hour. Pick any table you want. I'll bring some food and drinks out in a few minutes."

Pete nodded. "We'll go sit down."

Natalie took the opening to chime in. "Please don't feel obligated to make one of everything. We're fine with whatever you have planned for your guests. Please know how much I appreciate everything you've been doing for us."

Ashley walked around the counter and took Natalie's hands in hers. "You don't worry about any of that. I'm happy to help if it keeps you both safe. Rick has been a good friend to so many people in this town. I'm happy to finally be able to do something to help him. Now, go pick a table. I'll bring you some fresh-squeezed orange juice."

When they went out into the dining room, Shelly hurried to a table by the window. Natalie sat next to her and Pete took a seat across from them. Moments later, Ashley appeared with a tray carrying a glass pitcher of orange juice, a kettle full of coffee and a plate of cinnamon buns, filling the room with a delicious scent.

Ashley set everything down on the table. "The food will be out soon. I have to run to the garage to switch some laundry over. I'll be right back. Feel free to grab anything you need while I'm gone."

"Thank you." Pete nodded as she turned to leave.

Minutes later, when a burst of cool air rushed in, Pete looked up toward the front door. Natalie turned and saw a man coming in. Pete stood up, a smile on his face. That put Natalie at ease. He clearly knew this man and didn't see him as a threat.

"What brings you here this early?" Pete was walking toward him.

"Best breakfast in town. I come here a lot. Beats cooking for myself." The sound of his voice set Natalie's nerves on edge. She turned to get a better look at him. Then Shelly let out a gasp beside her. Her eyes were wide with fear.

Pete saw their reaction and tensed. That's when the man pulled out a gun.

"Don't reach for it, Pete."

Pete ignored the warning and pulled his Glock.

It was *him*. Natalie's stomach twisted into knots. Adrenaline rushed through her veins, tensing every muscle in her body. She grabbed Shelly's hand and ran through the kitchen door, her body shifting into autopilot. She didn't like the idea of leaving Pete behind with a gun pointed at him, but she had to put Shelly's well-being above all else. Pete had a gun of his own, which gave him a fighting chance. It was more than she had if that man ended up getting the upper hand.

Ashley must have still been working on the laundry.

She was nowhere in sight. They ran out the back door and into the woods. Natalie had no idea which direction to go. Nothing was familiar. She'd never ventured to this edge of town in the six months she'd been staying in the cottage. She stopped and tried to find something she recognized from when they walked to the B and B two days ago. Maybe she could retrace their steps to the hollow bushes where they'd hidden with Rick.

"Aunt Natty, that was the man! The one who was pushing the lady in the river! He's the one! Where will we go?" Shelly was on the verge of tears.

A gunshot echoed through the trees. She had no idea whose gun was fired. When another shot rang out, she and Shelly took off running deeper into the forest. She would look for a place to hide until help came. She just wasn't sure who was left to show up for them.

Hints of sunlight slipped over the horizon. Rick's eyelids were struggling to open. The pain radiating through his head was debilitating. When he realized someone was standing over him, he jerked away, unsure if it was the killer waiting to finish the job.

"Rick, it's me."

He squeezed his eyes closed and then open, trying to focus. It was Hazel. What a relief. He'd seen her go down when the gun went off next to his head.

"I thought he shot you."

"He did. He got my shoulder. A lot more painful than I imagined it to be." There was a bandage around the entire area, covering from her upper arm to her neck.

"Where is he? Did you get him?" Rick's vision was coming back into focus. Paramedics were working on the other officer near the porch. "How is he?"

Hazel crouched down in front of him. "He'll be fine. He was wearing a vest but he fell back and hit his head." She hesitated.

"What is it?" Rick pushed himself up on shaky legs.

Hazel stood up with him. "He got away. My phone broke when I fell. It took some time to get to a radio. I was in a lot of pain and bleeding." She paused again, which didn't sit well. "I haven't been able to reach Pete. It doesn't mean anything has happened. A squad car is going to check on them soon. There was another incident in town. The pharmacy was set on fire." She shifted awkwardly. "And he took our guns."

"Give me your keys." Rick had to get back to the B and B.

"What?"

"Your keys. Give me your keys."

"I can't drive like this. I can't lift my arm."

"You can stay here. Hazel, give me your keys." Rick held out his hand, palm up.

"I'm not supposed to..."

Rick was growing impatient. He was at the point of taking them by force if he had to. "I think the circumstances warrant a bend in the rules. Your boss could be hurt. I need to get over there. You know what the killer intends to do. We can't just sit here and do nothing. Another distraction in town? Come on. We know what's really happening."

Reluctantly, Hazel pulled the keys from her pocket and dropped them in his hand. "I'm going with you. This guy needs to be put away."

Rick didn't hesitate. He ran to the police cruiser. "Let's go. He could be there already."

At least the assailant hadn't flattened the tires this time.

He must have been in a rush. Rick drove faster than he ever had in his life, taking curves so fast he nearly spun out a few times. The dark road twisted back and forth, causing Hazel to grip the seat trying to keep from sliding around. She groaned a few times. Rick imagined she was in some pain with a bullet hole in her shoulder. It was a good thing it went all the way through. She would've had to go to the hospital if the bullet was still in her body. The more he thought about it, bringing Hazel along was probably a good idea. She was trained and pretty tough. He could use the backup. Even injured, she was more of a fighter than he'd realized. He'd seen it when Ray ran them off the road.

As the car shifted around the curves going down the mountain, all he could think of was Natalie and Shelly. They had to be alright. This was his plan and it completely blew up in his face. If anything happened to them or to Pete, he had no one to blame but himself.

When they reached Ashley's B and B, Rick flew into the small parking lot, skidding to a stop. There weren't any police cars there. Pete had purposely stayed without one to keep anyone from knowing he was there. Why weren't any other officers here yet? How bad was that fire? Rick jumped out and ran up the porch stairs and in through the front door, Hazel following behind, moving a little slower than normal with her injured shoulder.

Ashley looked startled when they came in. She was kneeling next to Pete, pressing a bloody towel to his side.

Hazel dropped down on her knees on Pete's other side. "Is it bad? Did you call an ambulance?"

"I'll be fine. He took my radio and my gun. He—"

"Where are they?" Rick interrupted. These details weren't important in the moment. Pete was well enough to talk. Now Rick wanted to know about the two people he'd promised to protect.

Pete shook his head, his eyes filled with regret. "I don't know. They ran out the back door when he came in. He followed after he shot me. It was..."

Rick didn't wait to hear anything else. He dashed through the kitchen and out the back door. The sky was beginning to lighten. It was easier to see but there was no way to know which way they had run. At the edge of the tree line, he stopped and listened. There was a faint sound of a man's voice. He ran into the trees, toward what sounded like talking. Maybe there was still a chance. Or maybe it wasn't even them. The reverberation of a gunshot propelled him forward. He couldn't be this close and then lose them. A scream echoed everywhere around him. He was pretty sure it was Shelly. And that they were down by the river. The question was, had the masked man just shot Natalie?

The bullet disappeared into the dirt directly in front of Natalie's feet. An inch closer and she might have lost some toes. She looked up at the man in front of her. Without a mask, he looked vaguely familiar. His voice was what made her certain that it was the same person who had attacked her in the cottage.

He was ranting, pacing back and forth. "You ruined everything I built here. I'll lose all of the money I invested in buying the store. I'll have to start over. Find another mark." She wasn't sure what he meant by that. He kept going. "If you could have kept that kid inside, she wouldn't have seen my face and none of this would have happened." He stopped walking back and forth and locked eyes with Natalie. There was so much rage in his glare.

Shelly was tucked behind her, shaking and whimpering. If they survived this, her niece was going to need help overcoming everything that had happened since that night down by the river. Natalie flinched when he took a step closer. He was still ten feet away, but the way he kept swinging that gun at his side made the distance feel useless. His finger kept rubbing against the trigger. He was clearly itching to pull it again. She had considered jumping into the river with Shelly, but without anything to help keep their heads above water, she wasn't sure she could keep Shelly from going under while trying to swim.

The dark-haired man raised the gun and pointed it at her. He seemed to be enjoying dragging this out. He tilted his head and watched her, like he'd done before. It was still a game to him. She decided she needed to buy some time. She could only hope that Ashley had found Pete and called for help by now.

"Did you hurt Rick?" She had to know.

He lowered the gun and smiled as he tilted his head the other way. He wasn't going to answer. He clearly liked the idea of letting her imagine the worst.

"You don't have to do this. Pete obviously knows you. You said you have to start over. Killing us won't change that. You can let us go. I don't know my way around these woods. You could be long gone before I find my way out."

His smile grew. "You think I would ever consider letting either of you live? That kid wrecked my life. Then you made it worse. You're both going to die before I go anywhere." He raised the gun again. His eyes narrowed. A hint of a smirk lifted one corner of his lips.

Natalie closed her eyes and reached her arms behind her, grasping Shelly. She began to pray. There was nothing else to be done. No way out of this. No one to stop this from happening. There was only God. If He was ready to take them, there was nothing to do but accept it. The sound of a gunshot halted her prayer and Natalie braced for impact.

She felt nothing.

A sudden commotion made her open her eyes. Rick was on the ground fighting the dark-haired man for the gun. She quickly looked down to check herself. She hadn't been shot. Turning, she saw Shelly hadn't been hit, either.

"Hide behind that tree. Quickly." Natalie pointed to a wide trunk nearby. Shelly ran and tucked herself out of sight.

Natalie watched the two men punching and grappling. They were both so fast. The gun was between them. She was terrified that Rick could be shot. Then the man swung his arm around to smash Rick in the face with the weapon, but Rick drove the blade of a pocketknife into the man's bicep. The weapon fell to the ground. Natalie quickly kicked it away. Then she ran over and picked it up. Holding it the way she'd seen others hold a gun, she yelled at them.

"Stop or I'll shoot you!" She tried to hold the weapon steady. It was hard to stop the trembling that was vibrating through her entire body. She'd been seconds from death a minute ago. Shelly would have been next.

Both men looked up at her. Rick quickly pulled away and stood up. He came to her side and rubbed her back.

"Let me have it. Everything is going to be okay now. Hand me the gun." His voice was calming. It helped her to finally feel like she could breathe again. When she released the gun into his hands, he pointed it at the man on the ground.

"Arnie, why?" Rick clearly knew him.

Shelly came running out from behind the tree. Natalie lifted her into her arms and held on tight. "It's over. You're safe now," she whispered in Shelly's ear, trying to soothe her.

The man Rick called Arnie glared up at him. "I let you live. I could have killed you more than once. The least you can do is give me the chance to get away. Show me the respect that I've shown you. We're cut from the same cloth. We see the world for what it really is."

"Never gonna happen. You think I would let you go? After everything you've done? What you were about to do?" There was fury in Rick's tone. His entire body was rigid. "We are nothing alike. You think that I would let you kill innocent people because we shared a few memories of our days in the military when I was in your store?"

Arnie shook his head. "I should've killed you. All you did was get in my way."

Hazel came running through an opening in the trees with three other officers. Two of them quickly secured Arnie with handcuffs while Hazel read him his rights. Then the officers pulled Arnie to his feet and started marching him back toward the B and B. Rick handed the gun to Hazel and told her what happened. Shelly wiggled out of Natalie's arms and stood next to her. She seemed to want to see what was going on now that Arnie had been taken away.

Hazel came over to Natalie. "Are either of you hurt? Do you need to go to the hospital?" When Natalie told her they were both fine, she looked relieved. "I'm glad. Really glad. We were worried when we couldn't reach Pete."

"Did that man shoot him?"

"He did but it went straight through without hitting any

major organs. He'll be fine." Hazel smiled. "He'll have a scar to show off now. He'll be insufferable."

Rick spoke up. "You can bet on that. Pete loves to tell a good war story."

Hazel nodded in agreement. "I'll need you guys to come in to give a formal statement. No rush. You can get cleaned up. Have something to eat. Get some rest. This afternoon is fine." She bent down a little and spoke to Shelly. "You should know that you saved that woman's life when you screamed down by the river the other night. She said she's alive because you were so brave." That seemed to lift Shelly's spirits a little. Hazel turned to Rick and Natalie. "I just heard that she came into the station this morning. One of us will fill you in on the details once we get the full picture."

Hazel started to walk away, then stopped and turned back to them. "Oh, Ashley said you're all welcome to stay in the B and B as long as you need to. There are some guests scheduled to check out today, so you'll be able to have separate rooms if you want. And another bit of good news—the bridge isn't as bad as they thought. It should be fixed in a few days." Then she headed up the trail.

It was finally over. Natalie felt like a ten-ton weight had been lifted off her shoulders. Rick was staring at her and Shelly, his eyes going back and forth between them. Then he lifted Shelly up, grabbed ahold of Natalie and pulled them into a tight embrace.

"I can't tell you how relieved I am that you're both safe. I was worried sick that I wouldn't get here in time." He squeezed tighter.

Natalie was really going to miss him. She had grown to care for him. She was so thankful that he wasn't hurt, or worse. For the first time in days, she allowed herself to let go and relaxed into his arms. The three of them stood there together, intertwined one last time. Natalie knew that there would be no reason for them to see each other once they both left Maple Rapids.

NINETEEN

It was three days later when Pete came to the B and B to tell Natalie and Rick that the bridge had been fixed. Natalie would finally be able to put Maple Rapids in her rearview mirror. She hadn't seen much of Rick in the last few days. She missed him being around but there was no sense in getting any more attached than she already was.

Ashley had volunteered to take Shelly into the kitchen while Natalie and Rick spoke to Pete. Ashley had been teaching her how to bake and promised they'd make Shelly's favorite cookies to take home with her.

Natalie and Rick sat at a round table in the dining room with Pete. He told them about the man who tried to kill them and the woman he tried to drown in the river.

"His real name is Daryl Cain. He was part of one of those survivalist militia groups. He was never actually in the military. Those stories were made up. He's a very skilled marksman and has extensive fight training, as you well know." He nodded toward Rick. "These people are hardcore. They hunt for their food. They don't recognize the government as an authority over them. The real Arnie Standish was a loner. Daryl killed him to assume his identity and take his life savings after stealing a stockpile of cash from his militia group.

"The woman is part of the group. She said Daryl was starting to complain. He didn't like the leader. Thought he could do better but no one agreed to back him. When he took off with the money they'd all saved to be there, she went looking for him. Apparently, she's some kind of tracker and used to be a PI. They just wanted the money back. She said they didn't care if he left the group.

"When she caught up with him, he told her to meet him by the river and he'd give her most of the money back if she promised not to blow his cover. When she got there, he had other plans. When Shelly screamed, she was able to push away from him. The current took her out of reach fast enough that Daryl couldn't catch her. She came forward because she knows he's dangerous. The group is well trained but they keep to themselves. I checked with local law enforcement and they've never been any trouble.

"Arnie was friendly with a lot of the officers in town. They had no idea he was the last person they should be sharing information with. If nothing else, they learned a valuable lesson. We'll be setting some strict rules about what they tell civilians after this. Not that they should have done it to begin with. But when he hit his own store to throw us off, no one suspected him. Especially with that limp."

"How did he run around like that? It gets worse when it rains." Rick leaned forward on his elbows.

"He must have faked the limp as part of his cover. It's the reason I didn't think to run a background check on him. He hasn't limped at all since he's been arrested. Another lesson learned." Pete leaned back in his chair.

"What now?" Natalie was stunned by how much damage this man had done.

"He'll be tried for multiple murders, among other

things. There's a long list of charges. The DA is going for the max here. Apparently, he's responsible for crimes in other states as well. I don't imagine he'll ever breathe free air again. He could even get the death penalty."

It was a relief to know he'd never be able to come after them again.

Pete stood up to leave and wished Natalie well. He told her that he hoped she would consider visiting Maple Rapids again. That it was normally a very peaceful place. She promised she'd think about it. When Rick walked him out, Natalie went into the kitchen to get Shelly. The tires on Natalie's car had been replaced. They didn't have any luggage to pack. It had all been lost in the motel fire. There was nothing left to do but say goodbye.

Ashely packed a large baggie of cookies for Shelly to take with her. She also wrote down the recipe so Shelly would be able to make them at home.

"I want to thank you for everything." Natalie took Ashley's hands in hers. "You've gone above and beyond. If you ever want to spend some time at the beach, you're always welcome to stay with us."

"I may take you up on that." Ashley kissed Shelly on the forehead and then hugged Natalie. "You take care of yourselves. You're always welcome here if you ever decide to come back." She took a step back. "I hope you do. I know someone who would want to see you again."

Was she referring to Rick?

"I don't know about that. He has other plans. I don't think he'll be around long." She took Shelly's hand. "What do you say to Ashley?"

"Thank you for the cookies."

"You are very welcome."

They walked out through the dining room and then the

living room. Rick was standing on the porch. In addition to being brave and selfless, he was one of the most handsome men Natalie had ever seen. His dirty blond hair fell across his forehead above those warm green eyes. His strong jaw shifted as he forced a smile.

"I guess you'll be going home now, huh?"

"I guess so. They held my job. I'll be back in my classroom next week." That had been a huge relief. "When do you leave for California?" She almost dreaded the answer.

"Not sure. Soon, I guess. I haven't finalized the details yet."

Natalie nodded. She wanted to get going. The thought of spending another minute in this town was too much. After everything that happened, she was about to lose the first man she'd ever felt a true connection with and there was nothing she could do about it but wish him well and thank him for all that he'd done.

"Well, we should be going." She walked down the stairs with Shelly at her side. She stopped next to her little SUV and turned to him. He came down the stairs. "Thank you. For everything. What you did for us…"

He waved it off. "Of course." He leaned down to Shelly. "Do you think I could have a hug before you go?" Shelly reached up and wrapped her arms around his neck. He stood up and held her. "You take care of your aunt when you get home."

"I will." Shelly giggled. "Do you want one of the cookies I baked with Ashley?"

"I would love one." He opened the back door and put Shelly down in the booster seat. Then he made sure her seat belt was firmly secured.

Shelly pulled a cookie out of the bag and handed it to him.

"Thank you." He took a bite. "This is the best cookie I have ever tasted." When she smiled, he closed the back door.

Natalie couldn't keep standing there in front of him. She would want to stay. To somehow convince him to pass on his dream job. She couldn't ask that of him. She quickly hugged him and then got into her car. She waved and then drove away. She watched him in the rearview mirror. He was just standing there, watching her leave. He wasn't trying to stop her. He clearly didn't feel the way she did. He was probably relieved to be rid of them.

When she turned onto the street and drove toward the bridge out of town, a hollow ache began to form in the pit of her stomach. At least Rick hadn't been hurt. She thanked God for that.

Natalie and Shelly were gone. It was harder than Rick thought it would be. He knew it was coming. He'd wanted to spend more time with them over the last few days but Natalie kept her distance. He supposed that made her feelings pretty clear.

Ashley came out and sat on the porch steps. "So did you tell her?"

"Tell her what?" Rick took a seat next to her.

"How you feel about her."

"What are you talking about?" He turned away, staring at the empty street at the end of the driveway.

"You know what I'm talking about. Why did you let her leave?" Ashley was always this way. She spoke her mind when she thought it would help.

"It's not like I had a choice. She couldn't wait to get out of here." He lowered his voice. "Away from me. I'm just a reminder of the worst experience of her life."

"I don't know about that."

He turned to her. "What do you mean?"

"The two of you should talk. It seems to be pretty obvious to everyone but you and Natalie that you belong together."

"I think you're misreading things." But what if Ashley was right? Should he have told Natalie how he felt? It didn't matter now. It was too late. He stood up. "I need to get packed up. And I need to book a flight. Besides, she barely said goodbye. I'm not sure she would have bothered if I hadn't been out here."

She nodded. "Or she thinks she's doing right by you by leaving. Just a thought. If you did want to talk to Natalie before you fly off, I have her address and phone number in my registration book. It's in the top left drawer of my desk."

"Why would I do that? She took off the second she could and didn't look back." He leaned against the railing. "You need to computerize this place. It would streamline things. Less work for you."

"I'm not doing that. Stop deflecting. Can you really tell me you're sure that's why she left so fast? I guess you know her better than I do. I should get back to work. See you inside." She got up and left him standing there to consider the possibilities.

Then reality dawned. Rick would never be anything but a bad reminder of Arnie Standish. Well, Daryl Cain. It was still hard to reconcile the man he'd gotten to know with who he really was. It was time for a fresh start. He needed to iron out the details of his new job and finally start moving forward. If nothing else, his time with Natalie and Shelly had helped him come to terms with what happened in the past. He was ready to start living.

TWENTY

Arriving in California last week felt like more of a mistake than the fresh start it was supposed to be. It wasn't that Rick's new employer in San Diego wasn't great. His first in-person meeting had gone very well. It wasn't that the weather wasn't as perfect as advertised, with most days landing around seventy degrees with clear skies. La Jolla, where Rick was planning to live, was a beautiful neighborhood lined with beaches and ocean bluffs. He should have been feeling pretty good by now. But Rick's sister was pregnant with her first child. He was going to miss so much being this far away from his family. If he was really being honest with himself, Ashley's words were still lingering and he couldn't help but wonder if he should have said something to Natalie before she left Maple Rapids.

As Rick walked through town, considering this new chapter in his life, he came across a small curved beach with big rocks that jutted out into the ocean. Seals and sea lions were sunbathing in the sand and along the rockline. His first thought was how excited Shelly would be if she was here to see this. He could almost hear the way Natalie would encourage Shelly's enthusiasm. An emptiness formed in the pit of his stomach. He missed them more than he should, considering how short their time together had been. Maybe the feeling would pass once he officially started the new job. It was possible that he was feeling these things because he had made such a big change so far from everything that was familiar to him.

He continued on his walk, taking in the stunning views of the water. He wondered if Natalie spent a lot of time on the beach in Spring Lake. There were still so many things he didn't know about her. So much he would want to experience with her. Or someone like her. The short time he'd spent with Natalie and Shelly had been transformative for Rick. It was difficult not to consider what years might be like with them in his life. But that wasn't what Natalie wanted. She'd avoided him after the danger ended. Then she rushed out of town as soon as Pete told her the bridge was fixed. He'd have to accept that he would have to find happiness with someone else. If that was even possible.

The curtains fluttered in the ocean breeze coming in through the windows. It had been a few weeks since leaving Maple Rapids. Natalie felt surprisingly at peace. She had been working on coming to terms with the source of her nightmares while trying to escape a killer. The realization that her brother and his wife had suffered the night they died was still a little difficult to accept. Now that she understood what was holding her captive in her dreams, sleep had become easier. The nightmares had finally stopped once she was back home.

Nearly dying so many times in the span of a few days had helped her realize that she wanted to move forward. Not just exist in grief. But actually start living again. She'd also learned a lot about who she was and what she wanted for herself. Getting to know Rick had given her closure about the way things ended with Eric. It was hard to imagine such a traumatic experience could be the source of so much personal growth. She supposed God did have a plan, even when things seemed bleak.

"Are you hungry?" Natalie found Shelly in the kitchen searching through the cabinets.

"Yes. I want to make more cookies."

"We can do that after dinner. I ordered a pizza. It'll be here any minute." Just then, the doorbell rang.

"I want to get it." Shelly went running.

"Wait for me." Natalie quickly followed.

When Shelly pulled the front door open, it wasn't the pizza delivery person standing on the porch. "Hey, Peanut."

Her niece squealed with delight and ran into Rick's arms. Natalie couldn't keep the smile from stretching across her face at the sight of him.

"What are you doing here? How did you know where we live?" She was stunned.

"I may have taken a peek in Ashley's registry book. I hope you don't mind."

"Of course not. Come in." She stepped aside.

Rick carried Shelly inside before he set her down. "Do you think you could give me a few minutes with your aunt?"

Shelly nodded. "I'll go get the ingredients out to make the cookies. We're baking after pizza. Will you stay and eat with us? Then you can help me bake."

"We'll see." Rick grinned at her. It was enough. She was off to the kitchen.

"Do you want to sit down?" Natalie gestured toward the couch as she sat near the end.

When Rick took a seat a little closer than she expected, Natalie couldn't help the swirl of excitement in her belly seeing him again. She had missed him so much more than she thought possible but she hadn't wanted to get in the way of his dream job in California. She couldn't help but wonder what he was doing here? Why he'd traveled this far to see her. Then she remembered that his family lived in Pennsylvania. Maybe he'd come to see them and her house was just close to something he was doing in the area. Given the kind of man he was, it was possible that he'd come by to check on them.

"Can I get you anything to drink?" Natalie's nerves were a little frazzled, but she didn't want it to show.

Rick shook his head. "No, thank you. The thing is... There are some things I wanted to say to you before you left Maple Rapids. I don't know why I didn't." He sat for a long moment without continuing.

Natalie waited, looking up at the intensity in his green eyes. "What did you want to tell me?" She couldn't imagine what he'd come all of this way to say.

"I know we only met a few weeks ago and we really only spent a few days together. But I feel like we got pretty close. I mean it was so easy being around you. Well, when we weren't running for our lives. Anyway, the company that offered me the job has a pretty big office in New York City. It wouldn't be that bad of a commute from here." Rick leaned closer and took her hands in his. "I found a furnished rental. I'd take it if you were interested in seeing if this could be more." His eyes locked with hers, waiting for her to say something.

"Are you sure you'd be happy doing that? I thought you really wanted to go out west?" She tried to keep from getting too excited. She needed to be sure first.

"What I wanted was a fresh start. I could have that here. With you and Shelly. My life feels empty without the two of you. Everywhere I went in California made me think of how you and Shelly would like it. How Shelly would get excited when I came across a beach filled with seals and sea lions. How you might be on the beach here while I walked in the sand there." He paused, seeming to try to find his words. "Everything feels empty without you there. Without Shelly. I miss her laughter. I miss…you. I miss being with you. Even with all of the bad things that happened, those days with you changed my life in ways I hadn't believed possible anymore. I know you may not feel the same way and I might just be a reminder of a really bad experience, but I'd like to see where this could go if you do."

There was no containing it anymore. "I've missed you every single day. I avoided you and left quickly because I knew I'd ask you not to go if I spent any time with you. I didn't want to get in the way of your dream."

Rick lifted his hand and slid his fingers along her cheek and into her hair. "You're my dream." He leaned forward and pressed his soft lips to hers. She could feel that kiss spark all the way down to her toes. When he pulled back, his gaze met hers. "You've healed my heart. I don't want to be away from you for another day. I love you, Natalie. And I love Shelly. I want to give us a chance to see where it will lead. Honestly, I don't have any doubts that we'll be great together. If you say yes, I'll move here and take the job in New York."

Natalie couldn't contain her smile. "Yes. I would like that very much. Being with you in those calmer moments was just as healing for me. The man you are helped me see what had been missing, even before I lost my brother.

I wanted you to be part of God's plan for me. I want you in our lives. If you'll be happy here, I want you to stay. I love you, too."

Rick pulled her closer. "I can't imagine anything that would make me happier." He leaned in and kissed her again. It was slow and gentle. Natalie could feel the love between them.

Just as their lips parted, Shelly came in and stood in front of Rick. "C'mon. I need you to get some things down from the high cabinet. I'm too short."

Rick turned to Natalie and gave her one more quick kiss before he stood up. Natalie reached for his hand.

"I'm going to want to hear more about that beach with the seals." Natalie smiled as Rick pulled her to her feet.

"I'd rather take you to see it for yourself. When the time is right, I'll take you both to San Diego to see everything that reminded me of you."

"Where is San Diego?" Shelly grabbed Rick's hand and tugged him toward the kitchen.

Rick smiled and followed Shelly. "It's in California."

"Where is that? It sounds far."

Natalie listened to the banter between them. Rick was so good with Shelly. Having him here filled her heart with more joy than she would have expected. She was happier than she'd been in a very long time. The best part was that Rick didn't make her feel like she needed to be anybody but exactly who she was.

EPILOGUE

A lazy ocean wave rolled over his toes, sinking his feet farther into the wet sand. Rick was watching Natalie help Shelly build a sandcastle on the beach. It had been nearly a year since he'd moved to Spring Lake. Definitely the best decision of his life. Being with these two amazing people filled his life in ways he hadn't even known he needed.

Shelly came running over and took his hand. She was so spirited and full of mischief in the best possible way. He loved her like she was his own daughter. "Is it time?" She blinked those thick black lashes up at him.

"Time for what?" Natalie stood up and brushed the sand from her legs.

"I think it is." Rick reached into his pocket and palmed what he needed.

"What are you two up to?" Natalie smiled, looking back and forth between Rick and Shelly. This was becoming a regular thing. They tended to get into mischief together, keeping Natalie amused with their silly antics.

Rick dropped down on one knee and opened the little velvet box in his hand. "Natalie, I love you with my whole heart. I can't imagine my life without you and Shelly in it. I want to spend every day showing you what you mean to me." A tear tipped over her bottom lid and slid down her tanned skin. Her smile told him the answer before he even asked the question. "Natalie Owens, will you marry me?"

She nodded, tears streaming down both cheeks. "Yes."

He slipped the ring onto her finger and stood up. He held her face in his hands and kissed her before pulling her into his arms. When Shelly wrapped herself around both of them, they parted and pulled her between them. They had become a family in spite of all of the terrible things they'd gone through. Rick thanked the Lord for making this possible. For giving him his heart's desire.

* * * * *

*If you liked this story from Addie Ellis,
check out her previous Love Inspired Suspense book:*

Hunted in the Mountains

Find more great reads at www.LoveInspired.com.

Dear Reader,

Thank you for taking the time to read *Hiding from Danger*. I hope you enjoyed going on this journey with Natalie and Rick. Losing people sometimes makes it difficult to continue moving forward. For soldiers it can often be survivor's guilt or a sense of failure. For others the loss is usually a loved one. When caught in a cycle of grief, it can be difficult to recognize that there might be a deeper cause or that a perceived personal sense of responsibility may be misplaced. The act of helping others can sometimes shift that perspective because it is usually less difficult to be objective with someone other than yourself. This can help open the mind to see your own troubles more clearly. While we may not always understand God's plan, we can always turn to Him in times of need.

Wishing you well on your journey,
Addie Ellis

Get up to 4 Free Books!

We'll send you 2 free books from each series you try PLUS a free Mystery Gift.

FREE Value Over **$25**

Both the **Love Inspired®** and **Love Inspired® Suspense** series feature compelling novels filled with inspirational romance, faith, forgiveness and hope.

YES! Please send me 2 FREE novels from the Love Inspired or Love Inspired Suspense series and my FREE gift (gift is worth about $10 retail). After receiving them, if I don't wish to receive any more books, I can return the shipping statement marked "cancel." If I don't cancel, I will receive 6 brand-new Love Inspired Larger-Print books or Love Inspired Suspense Larger-Print books every month and be billed just $7.19 each in the U.S. or $7.99 each in Canada. That is a savings of 20% off the cover price. It's quite a bargain! Shipping and handling is just 50¢ per book in the U.S. and $1.25 per book in Canada.* I understand that accepting the 2 free books and gift places me under no obligation to buy anything. I can always return a shipment and cancel at any time by calling the number below. The free books and gift are mine to keep no matter what I decide.

Choose one:
- ☐ **Love Inspired Larger-Print** (122/322 BPA G36Y)
- ☐ **Love Inspired Suspense Larger-Print** (107/307 BPA G36Y)
- ☐ **Or Try Both!** (122/322 & 107/307 BPA G36Z)

Name (please print)

Address   Apt. #

City   State/Province   Zip/Postal Code

Email: Please check this box ☐ if you would like to receive newsletters and promotional emails from Harlequin Enterprises ULC and its affiliates. You can unsubscribe anytime.

Mail to the Harlequin Reader Service:
IN U.S.A.: P.O. Box 1341, Buffalo, NY 14240-8531
IN CANADA: P.O. Box 603, Fort Erie, Ontario L2A 5X3

Want to explore our other series or interested in ebooks? **Visit www.ReaderService.com or call 1-800-873-8635.**

---

*Terms and prices subject to change without notice. Prices do not include sales taxes, which will be charged (if applicable) based on your state or country of residence. Canadian residents will be charged applicable taxes. Offer not valid in Quebec. This offer is limited to one order per household. Books received may not be as shown. Not valid for current subscribers to the Love Inspired or Love Inspired Suspense series. All orders subject to approval. Credit or debit balances in a customer's account(s) may be offset by any other outstanding balance owed by or to the customer. Please allow 4 to 6 weeks for delivery. Offer available while quantities last.

Your Privacy—Your information is being collected by Harlequin Enterprises ULC, operating as Harlequin Reader Service. For a complete summary of the information we collect, how we use this information and to whom it is disclosed, please visit our privacy notice located at https://corporate.harlequin.com/privacy-notice. Notice to California Residents – Under California law, you have specific rights to control and access your data. For more information on these rights and how to exercise them, visit https://corporate.harlequin.com/california-privacy. For additional information for residents of other U.S. states that provide their residents with certain rights with respect to personal data, visit https://corporate.harlequin.com/other-state-residents-privacy-rights/.

LIRLIS25